STALKED

She froze for exactly one moment, and then ran, with a shriek. Gravity just kept on pulling the thing down after her, terrifying and enormous. At the last possible moment, she swung herself over the landing and out of the way.

She took a deep breath.

Whoever had killed Lynn Rivers had just tried to kill again!

To Lindsay, this book
was meant to be a
christmas present but we
did not get to the bookstore
until May 1st 93!

much love   Mum

Dying to Know

JEFF HAMMER

AN AVON  FLARE BOOK

DYING TO KNOW is an original publication of Avon Books. This work has never before appeared in book form. This work is a novel. Any similarity to actual persons or events is purely coincidental.

AVON BOOKS
A division of
The Hearst Corporation
1350 Avenue of the Americas
New York, New York 10019

Copyright © 1991 by Donald Maass
Published by arrangement with Donald Maass Literary Agency
Library of Congress Catalog Card Number: 91-91774
ISBN: 0-380-76143-2
RL: 6.7

First Avon Flare Printing: July 1991

AVON FLARE TRADEMARK REG. U.S. PAT. OFF. AND IN OTHER COUNTRIES, MARCA REGISTRADA, HECHO EN U.S.A.

Printed in the U.S.A.

RA 10 9 8 7 6 5 4 3 2 1

DYING TO KNOW

a column by
Diane Delany

Hi there, sports fans!

You're in the wrong place!

This isn't the sports page, folks! That's on the *back* of the paper! This here's the *gossip* column, and don't you forget it. And just in case you watched too many soap operas on summer vacation and got a bad case of amnesia, I'm your faithful reporter, Diane Delany, serving up the latest juicy tidbits of Maxville sociological and anthropological study!

But first, a word from our sponsor.

Gossip can be fun. But it *can* be hurtful too. I try to keep it clean and sweet, gentle readers. But there are those among us who have spread a lot of dirt.

Particularly the trio I call the Evil Sisters.

Hi out there, witches! You know who you are!

1

BEFORE

JIM STEVENS

Klepto.

Kleptomaniac.

Definition: an individual with a compulsion to steal.

Jim Stevens had been that way, once. He thought about that every morning as he stopped to get coffee at his neighborhood 7-Eleven. Even as he dumped his two packets of sugar and a glunk of half-and-half into the Styrofoam cup now, he looked down the aisle at the candy section. Two years ago, in another school, another life, he would have walked away with a half-dozen candy bars in his pocket, unpaid for.

Jim sipped at the bittersweet brew as he brought it around to the counter. Dawn was just creeping in through the windows, and Jim knew that he was going to be in plenty of time not only to open the school store that morning, but also to do some restocking. He took another gulp of hot coffee and let the drink wake him up some.

"Seventy cents," said the oriental gentleman behind the counter.

Jim Stevens counted out change from hi[s]
There were some donuts at the school store
from yesterday. Those would be his break[fast]
counted out two quarters and two dimes. What a
rush! Actually paying for stuff, with money he
earned himself!

He went out to his old Ford, zipping his jacket up
against the bracing fall morning, got into the car,
and drove to Maxville High School. He parked
around back and Bill Hickey, the night maintenance
man, let him in.

"Early!"

"Yeah. Gotta restock!"

"Jeez, Jim, I could use a guy like you! You want
a full-time job, you let me know!"

"Thanks, man. I really appreciate the thought."

The trust! They *trusted* him! They liked him! Jim
felt a little thrill at the base of his spine as he opened
the lock of the walk-in-closet-sized room that served
as the Maxville High school store. He turned on the
light, found the donut box, ate a honey-dip, washed
it down with half the sixteen-ounce cup of 7-Eleven
coffee, and then got down to work. There were boxes
of pens, pencils, and notebook paper that needed to
be opened and put up on shelves.

Jim was a slender guy with blue eyes and limp
blond hair, the kind who looked good in wire-rim
glasses—like a sensitive poet. He'd even tried wearing wire rims, and he'd tried poetry, but it just
wasn't him. Mostly, he just wanted to get his life
together here in Maxville. He'd been here a little
over a year now, and things were going well, really
well. At seventeen, he was a senior. B average. He'd
probably attend the area community college and then

3

jump up to State, but that was just fine with him. After all the shoplifting back in California, and all the therapy and all the grief he'd caused his parents and himself, he was happy just to have a normal quiet life, where people respected him, where people *trusted* him.

As Jim set out a new batch of erasable Bics on the metal display tree on the counter, the dream came back to him, the dream he'd had last night.

The nightmare.

The hand on his shoulder, the angry voices, the police, the whispers and cries. "Thief! Thief!" But this was not the past, he'd realized in the middle of the dream. This was now!

And everybody knew! All his friends, his teachers! They'd never ever trust him again!

Tense, he went and drank the rest of the coffee. Then he went and set up the cash register for the morning's receipts. He worked here forty-five minutes before homeroom, at lunch period, and then a half hour after school. It wasn't a lot of money as part-time jobs went, but his father, a prominent if new member of the community, had talked the principal into getting it for him so that Jim could meet his fellow classmates more easily. The first year had worked out very well, so Jim was set for the job for his senior year as well. His biggest fear last year was that someone would unearth the truth about his past. By the end of the year he'd relaxed a bit. Maybe *too* much. He'd told someone . . . someone he was dating . . . they'd stopped dating and now he regretted the confession.

The dreams had started.

He shrugged it off and finished restocking. Better

to think about that biology quiz today, run through the stuff he had committed to memory, and restock the phylum names whose slots were empty!

The coffee was long since finished, the bell had rung, and the supply of number two pencils was threatened with depletion, when Mr. Ricker, the business-ed. teacher who oversaw the school store operation, came by about ten minutes before homeroom. He had with him a young girl with glasses on. Phoebe Williams, if Jim's memory served.

"Jim," said Mr. Ricker, adjusting his Coke-bottle-thick glasses, "Phoebe's going to spell you for a bit. I want to buy you a cup of coffee in the teacher's lounge."

"I just had a cup, Mr. Ricker. That's about all I—"

Mr. Ricker didn't smile, and Jim's heart sank. "You can have a Coke, then." Something felt wrong.

Jim allowed himself to be guided down the hall to the lounge. Maybe something *wasn't* wrong. Maybe he was going to get a raise! Maybe Mr. Ricker was going to give him the coveted manager job, which carried academic credits and kudos with it.

However, one more look at Mr. Ricker's stern balding features told him that neither was in the cards.

"Jim, you've been a good worker. I've got no complaints. When you applied for another year, I gladly accepted you because you worked so hard last year. However, as time progresses, I realize I made a mistake. Other deserving students need the opportunity, and maybe I should have left you free to

5

pursue other part-time work, to—er, expand your resumé."

Jim blinked. His Coke sat before him, untouched and forgotten. "Mr. Ricker? You're *firing* me?"

"No. Not really. I am giving you an opportunity for movement here—"

"I *like* working at the store!"

"Others would like to work at the store," said Mr. Ricker brusquely. "I made a mistake. Of course, I'll be glad to give you a strongly positive letter of reference. . . ."

His fear was turning to anger. He felt a sick churning emotion in his stomach. "That's not true! You're not telling me the whole story, are you?"

Mr. Ricker looked away. "I don't know what you mean, Jim."

At that point he knew instinctively that he'd been right. So what was to hide? "You know about the shoplifting."

Mr. Ricker sighed. "I heard a rumor. I can't afford the chance, Jim. We've had troubles with this before, and if there's another . . . well, I have my own position at this school to worry about. Yes, I heard a rumor, and I took the liberty of ascertaining its truth."

"I've been a *great* worker! I haven't stolen anything!" Jim shouted.

"I'm not accusing you of anything, Jim. I've said nothing about this to anybody. I'm sorry, but I just can't take the chance!"

"But if there's a rumor . . . if you fire me . . . everyone will think it's true!"

"Refer anyone who says anything to me. The story will be that you decided to move on. You

6

needed more social life. Whatever you choose to say, I will back it up." Mr. Ricker looked him directly in the eye, firmly and authoritatively. "However, I *cannot* allow you to continue working at the store anymore."

"Okay," said Jim. "I understand." The bell rang. "I have to go get my books."

"I'm giving you two weeks' severance, Jim, and whatever moral support you need. I just ask you for your understanding here."

"Yeah."

Jim got up, got his books back at the store. The new girl already looked as though she *owned* the place. A feeling of deep grief filled him, and he struggled to hold back the tears as he left the store that he had run so well.

It's *her* fault, he thought as he trudged toward his homeroom. I should never have told her.

He honestly had thought he could trust her.

The thing was he hadn't really known that she was part of such a gossip-mongering clique. . . . She'd seemed so sweet, he thought.

As he traipsed along the noisy hallways, the fresh scents of students' perfumes and colognes passing him, the clatter of banging locker doors filling his ears, he imagined that people were staring at him, whispering to each other, "There he goes! The klepto! The shoplifter! *Nobody* will trust *him* now! He's got problems. *Big* problems!"

As fate would have it, just before he reached his homeroom, he saw her.

Lynn Rivers.

He saw her walking along the hall, hugging a load

of her books, with her best buddies, Melissa Birch and Toni Ayers.

The Evil Sisters, the school paper gossip column called them. Yes, that they were.

And as they passed by, they didn't even acknowledge Jim Stevens's presence, cold witches that they were!

Not even Lynn. He'd really cared for her, thought Jim, moping into his homeroom class just as the bell rang, and dumping his books on his desk. And how does she reward him?

Betrayal!

He sat in his homeroom, rage slowly rising in him as the teacher went about the business of calling the roll. He hardly noticed the buzz of conversation around him, the chatter, the gossip.

No, he was too intent on his anger.

The announcements over the PA system commenced.

"And don't forget," the announcer was saying, "to pick up your new copy of this week's edition of the Maxville *Trumpet*, featuring your favorite gossip column, 'Dying to Know,' written by our own Town Mouth, Diane Delany!"

By the time the bell rang again, releasing the students to their classes, all Jim Stevens could think about was how *furious* he was at Lynn Rivers.

She'd ruined his life!

And all he could think about as he burned down the hall was how much he'd like to get his hands around that pretty throat.

About how much Lynn Rivers deserved to *die!*

8

DYING TO KNOW

a column by
Diane Delany

... so it looks like little Goldilocks is happy with her Big Bear at last.

Not to get lost in the shuffle, may I add that Yours Truly, Mini-Mouth, is *still* quite happy with her wonderful boyfriend, Adam "Isn't He Gorgeous" Grant?

On a more somber note, I must say that I have learned that those Siblings of Sin are up to no good again. And I do mean the Evil Sisters I spoke about in my last column. Gossip is one thing. Slander is another.

Stop it, ladies, before somebody *really* gets hurt!

BEFORE

HEATHER PERKINS

"Hey, babe!" said the college guy, sauntering up to the table in the crowded restaurant. He looked varsity or fraternity or something college jocky, with a roll to his shoulders and a jaunty curl to his lip. He was the kind of guy that Heather Perkins seemed to be attracting lately. A type that wasn't *her* type at all. "You're Heather Perkins, aren't you?"

She wished she could lie and say she wasn't. But she'd always tried to make a practice of being truthful, even with jerks like this. "Yes. That's right."

The guy put a hand on the cushioned top of the booth and leaned over. Heather got a noseful of cheap Sex Musk cologne and recycled beer. "You're just as cute as they say. How about a date?"

"I'm sorry. I'm *on* a date."

"Ah, dump him." The guy jabbed a couple of thumbs toward himself, Andrew Dice Clay–style. "I'm the kind of man that a woman like *you* wants."

"The kind of man . . . what's *that* supposed to mean?" She had a terrible feeling about this.

It was happening again!

"The kind of guy who can *satisfy* you, babe! The

10

kind of guy who can give you the sort of action I hear you crave!''

The jerk was looking back, as though grandstanding for a bunch of buddies.

"You don't know me! How do you know what I crave?" said Heather, feeling herself blush with anger and shame despite herself.

The guy honestly looked surprised. He blinked and seemed a bit embarrassed. Clearly this cold, harsh reception was not what he'd expected. "Ummmm . . . story is, among some of the guys, that you like jocks and you're real . . . uhmm . . . friendly.''

"And who told them *that?!*" Heather craned her neck. Sure enough, there were a bunch of college guys, laughing and carrying on. Along with them Heather recognized three girls. Toni Ayers. Melissa Birch.

And Lynn Rivers, her former friend. Her former *confidante*.

Heather understood now.

"They, just, uh, heard it." He was caught in midproposition, so he couldn't bow out gracefully. "So how about it then?"

"No. And tell your so-called friends they're *wrong*. I'm *not* friendly. Buzz off!''

"Sheesh. What's your problem?"

The guy left.

"Friendly." What that jock had meant was "available." Heather Perkins was sixteen years old and a junior in high school. Up until the age of fifteen she'd been skinny as a rail and flat as a board. During her fifteenth year, however, she'd . . . developed. She'd "filled out" as her uncle Al had said

11

admiringly upon seeing her after a two-year absence from the area.

It helped (or rather, in this kind of case *didn't* help) that her long hair was a beautiful shiny shade of auburn and her eyes were deep brown, her nose was perky, and she had great cheekbones. With a body like hers was now, she could make a potato sack look sexy, and Lynn Rivers had taught her to wear much nicer clothes than that. But then, when Lynn's buddies Toni and Melissa had invited her to join their "clique" and "be popular" and she'd refused (she'd always loathed Toni and Melissa and their vicious gossip) suddenly Lynn started paying less attention to her and the rumors started.

The rumors that she was "easy."

Ted Hamilton trotted up (finally!) from his trip to the boys' room. "So, you want some ice cream too, Heather?" he asked sheepishly. He looked funny with that stubborn lock of red hair hanging down over his forehead. Thank heavens for guys like Ted, who liked her just for herself and not for her body or her reputation, erroneous as that might be.

"I want," said Heather, still flushed despite herself, "to get *out* of here!"

On the way out, Lynn Rivers looked her way. Heather flashed her a frown. Lynn looked away.

Toni and Melissa laughed, and the college boys laughed with them.

"Why are we stopping?"

"I thought we could talk a little bit, Heather."

"You can't talk while you drive?"

"Not and chew gum and rub my stomach too!"

Heather laughed. Ted could be pretty funny some-

12

times. They'd been driving along Oakwood Park in his parents' Mazda, and he'd just pulled off into a parking section by some picnic tables. It was nice, what with the moon up and the wind soughing through the trees, knocking off the fall-touched leaves. The park smelled of dead camp fires and of fresh grass, and pleasant childhood memories sprang to mind.

"What do you want to talk about, Ted?"

"This is what, our third date, Heather?"

"Yes, that's right."

"I've enjoyed going out with you. A lot."

"You've been fun too, Ted."

A funny kind of excitement fluttered in her abdomen. She wondered what kind of feelings this guy had for her! She liked him, that was for sure, in a very nice way. And, boy, was it great to have someone to do things with, a guy who could be your friend when you're giving off major attracting scents and former friends are pointing the dogs in your direction.

"Thanks. I try. Sometimes, though . . ."

"Yes, Ted?"

"Sometimes I get the feeling that I'd like, to, uh, you know . . . uh . . . get affectionate."

Heather smiled. Despite what Lynn and her hooligan hell sisters said, she hadn't had a whole lot of experience with kissing, much less anything else. And Ted *did* smell awfully nice. Old Spice and leather? That's what it smelled like he was wearing. He had on a leather jacket and his clothes were neat and freshly pressed, and his hair did look like fun to touch.

So I'll let him kiss me. That's all.

"I guess you've been so nice, you've earned a kiss, Ted." *And that's all!* she thought her phrasing implied.

He seemed so shy about it that she figured that he was pretty safe. Besides, it wasn't as though she wasn't *human*. Just because she wasn't the slut the so-called Evil Sisters claimed she was didn't mean she didn't like guys!

Tentatively, he leaned over toward her. Just his face. Lips puckered, presumably. She had to laugh to herself at his awkwardness, but it *was* awfully sweet!

Their lips met. He tasted of a Tic Tac. They kind of pressed their faces together for a while, and it wasn't anything electric, but it *was* rather pleasant. He put his arm around her back, brushing her neck with his sleeve.

Oooh. Nice.

She was just starting to enjoy herself, when suddenly things got kind of out of hand.

Suddenly, she had *two* tongues in her mouth.

And then she had a hand fumbling with the buttons on her blouse.

"Mmpph!" she said.

Without warning, the car seat went over, and she went with it, Ted along for the ride. Before she could say or do a thing, he was on top of her, all *over* her!

"Hey! Ted! What . . . for heaven's sake, *stop!* I said just a kiss! What do you think I am!"

"Bill Evans and some of the other guys on the football team say that you're *dynamite!*"

"Ted! NO!"

"They said you always say that at first, but then you give in. Especially if you go out with a guy

14

three times. So let's have some fun! I think you're so sexy, I can't stand it!''

With every last bit of her energy, she pushed him off and back into his own seat of the car. "You're going to have to stand it, Ted. Take me home, right now!''

"Aw, come on, Heather. I mean, it's not like you've never done it before. Like with *dozens* of other guys! And we actually *like* each other!''

Again he put his hand on her, this time on her thigh. Uncomfortably far up.

She slapped him.

Then she opened the door.

"Not anymore, Ted!''

She slammed the door in a white-hot blaze of anger and began walking across the park. She lived only about a mile away, and she'd rather hoof it than spend one more second with that *rat* in sheep's clothing. And he'd seemed so gentle and nice before. Guys! Were they all the same! Did they all think with their reproductive equipment?

As she walked, she didn't cool down.

Those girls. Those *witches!* This was all their fault.

She felt helpless tears streaming down her face.

Her life was ruined here in Maxville. Totally *ruined!*

She wanted to *kill* them. She wanted them all *dead!*

Especially the one she'd trusted, the one who she'd once thought of as a friend, even a mentor.

Lynn Rivers.

DYING TO KNOW

a column by
Diane Delany

... was that really Harriet and Martin I spotted snuggling in the new bleachers during the game? Is this an item here, or were they just two concerned students contributing toward our beloved Principal's promise of a "kinder, gentler" set of Maxville fans after last year's hilarious Basketball Riots.

A Note to the Sisters: These painful lies you've been spreading *have* hurt. I know at least two cases now of *real agony!* Please, please, *seriously*.

STOP!

Or Yours Truly will have to take Personal Measures!

BEFORE

RICK ELKINS

He could feel their eyes boring into the back of his neck.

Crazy, they were thinking. Nutcase. A loony.

And: jeez, that guy must have *problems!*

Rick Elkins walked down the Maxville High lunchroom aisle, picking up a sub sandwich and three cartons of low-fat milk along the way. He paid at the register and then carried his tray over to a table that wasn't occupied. He felt like being alone this lunch period. He needed to study anyway.

Ignore it, man. They don't know anything. They don't know about that stay in the psychiatric hospital this summer. They don't know about your old man. They don't know you're on antidepressant medication. All they know is that the star defensive linebacker didn't go into training this August, and he ain't on the team in his senior year. That's all they know, so don't be so darned *paranoid!*

He examined the sandwich with trepidation. Salami, bologna, American cheese, the barest spray of onion and lettuce, a measly wilted tomato, and a lonely little slice of pepperoni. They call this a submarine

17

sandwich, huh? Well, it was probably better than what he got in the hospital, anyway.

He chomped into it, hardly noticing what it tasted like.

Rick Elkins was squat and powerfully built, which stood him in good stead on the football field. He just wished he were as steady and solidly built emotionally and psychologically. He felt better now, *much* better, if feeling not much of anything was really better. That's what Prolax did to you; it kind of stripped you of emotions for a while. Just long enough to let your insides mend, taper you off, Rick . . . and then we'll take you on the road to full recovery. You'll be slugging balls out of the park by spring, take my word for it.

Yeah. Sure. Right now, he just wanted to slug his old man. And his mom wasn't any gem either, but he didn't want to hurt her. Least he hadn't gotten violent. Those raging fights through the summer . . . the family turmoil. That's what had tilted him over the edge. Things went dark then, real dark, and only in the hospital had he begun to see any hint of light. . . .

He pulled the English textbook from under his arm, opened it to the assigned Ernest Hemingway story, and started to read.

"Yo! Elkins! Okay if we sit here?"

He looked up. Towering over him, even across the fold-down table, were Tim Rodriguez and Matt Matthewson. Left guard. Fullback. Maxville High football team.

"Looks like there are plenty of seats, guys." He went back to the story.

18

A whiff of peanut butter and jelly wafted across the table.

"Working hard, working hard!"

"Funny. You'd think with all that free time on his hands, now—what with no football and everything, he wouldn't have to study at lunchtime."

"Yeah. Maybe take some time and talk to his old buddies."

A twinge moved deep inside Rick, below the anti-depressant. Buddies? These guys were *never* his friends. They always gave him a hard time. Which was probably what they were giving him now.

He looked up, wearing a questioning look. "You guys get brain transplants or something? You're not Rodriquez and Matthewson anymore?"

"He talks!"

"He lives!"

They laughed. Another twinge. A small pang of hurt bubbled briefly in him. He ignored it. "Yeah. I'm still alive."

"So tell us true, Elky boy. How come no fool's ball this year? You were maybe looking at a college scholarship!" said Matthewson.

"I'm saving up my energy for baseball! I'm hittin' the books. Gotta get my grade average up or there ain't *gonna be* no college."

"Smart. Real smart. For you. But you know, man, we were kinda countin' on you. Hate to say it, but we're kinda hurtin' this year," said Rodriquez.

Honest enough. That deserved a direct answer. He looked Rodriquez square in the eye. "I'm real sorry about that. I know I let you guys down. But, honestly, I don't think I'd have been a good player for the team this year. I have to get stuff squared away

19

first. I had a great year last year and as pains in the neck as you guys are, you're good players and you helped. Thanks. This year—well, again, what can I say. Sorry."

He looked down at his sandwich. He suddenly lost his appetite.

"Maybe he's right, man," said Matt. "Maybe a guy who spent time in the bughouse wouldn't be able to stay on his feet anyway."

"Matt!"

Rick looked up. A queasy terror gripped him in the gut. It was like the Prolax suddenly had worn off, and he could feel things he wasn't supposed to feel.

And they didn't feel good.

"Ooops!" But Matthewson was grinning.

They knew. And if these goons knew, then, if the whole school didn't know, it soon would. But how had they found out? He tried to keep it so quiet. The doctors had assured him that his visit would be a secret. And the cover story that had gone out was that he'd gone to work at a relative's summer camp in Vermont.

"What a doofus!" said Rodriquez. He turned to Rick. "Apologies for the mouth that ate Cleveland, Elkins."

"Yeah! I guess we all get *depressed* sometimes. Hey, you know, I always wondered what those pills are like, man. Can I try some? Might help with the way I feel about this crummy football season!"

God! They knew everything. They probably even knew about his old man!

He tried to open his mouth, tried to say something clever, something macho, but he couldn't even get a syllable out. Fortunately he was able to keep an expressionless facade. They couldn't see the weak, terrified feelings that were rolling around inside him.

"What you need is some cleats in your face," said Rodriguez to Matthewson.

"Okay. As long as Elkins gets to do it. He probably doesn't have the energy. He's so *depressed!*"

He felt like decking the guy, but that wouldn't solve anything. They'd just both get suspended. No, maybe last year he might have punched Matt, but today he kept himself in check. He let the medicine do its work, and in fact, it helped some.

"Look," he managed, "we can't all be as well adjusted as you, Matthewson. Or maybe it helps to get hit in the face with the ball a lot!"

The guys laughed. Good. Good, man. Keep it up. Jocular, macho. That was the ticket. That hid the pain.

"You seem okay, man."

He shrugged. "I had some trouble. I got sick. A psychological flu, okay? I'm gettin' better. Besides, maybe you don't want me around the showers in this condition now, anyway."

He made knifing motions and psycho-shriek sounds, playing Tony Perkins. The guys laughed at that one, too. Good. Very good!

"Well, at least you got a sense of humor about it," said Matt.

"Kinda," said Rick. "It wasn't any fun. And I really didn't want anybody to know about it, you know what I mean?"

"Can't blame you for that!" said Rodriguez.

"So—uhm—just how did you find out?"

"What—about your nervous breakdown?" said Rodriguez.

"He sure don't look nervous to me, now," said Matthewson. "He kind of looks turned off!"

"Shut up, man. It's the Age of Anxiety. Of course, it takes brains to worry." Rodriguez turned back to Rick. "Who did we hear it from? It's hard to say."

Unbelievable! It was all over town!

Matthewson folded his arms over his chest and looked at Rick skeptically. "Come on! Where do you think we got it from. From where *all* the dirt comes from!"

Rick flinched. "Not from that stupid gossip column in the paper."

"What? Diane D.'s piece of fertilizer? Heck no— Let's just say that three very blabby but foxy babes have been shooting off their mouths as usual."

Rick swallowed. Ice seemed to drift down his spine. He knew exactly who they were talking about, and he knew *why*.

For some reason, at the end of last year, right in the middle of his whole life going down the tubes, Melissa Birch had started getting interested in him. She hinted stuff about the junior prom and wondering if she would see him at the ballgame and made complimentary noises about his athletic prowess. He didn't even realize until he thought about it later, after the worst nightmare of his life was over and he'd come out of it alive, that she'd been coming on to him. So *that* was why she'd been so cold to him after he hadn't responded. She thought he'd turned her down, when the truth was, romance was the *last* thing that had been on his mind.

Anger bubbled up below his sedate surface. She and Lynn Rivers and Toni Ayers somehow must have suspected that he wasn't in Vermont. They must have dug up that info.

He managed to chew the fat with the guys just long enough so that they saw him as being okay. But he wasn't okay. He excused himself, dumped what was left of his sandwich, went off to the men's room, and threw up in one of the stalls.

Wiping his face off with a damp towel, he looked up at his face in the mirror, and what he saw there was cold, hard hatred.

Everybody knew now.

He thought the worst of the pain was over, but really it had just begun.

Those girls . . .

Those blasted girls . . .

They were going to *pay!*

DYING TO KNOW

a column by
Diane Delany

... and no one was more surprised than your faithful reporter to learn that *that* dynamic duo had gone solo.

... and stop the press, dear readers. My little chirping gossip canary has just been twittering again. Seems that a certain Terrible Trio who have visited this column before have once more been disseminating information faultier than Southern California. Watch out what drops from these ladies' lips—the droppings from my gossip canary have more value!

BEFORE

Perfect!

Hedda Hopper, eat your heart out! There was a new queen of gossip in the world!

Diane finished keyboarding the last sentence of her gossip column into the IBM computer, smiled to herself, and then saved the file. She swept back the brunette bangs that had fallen into her green eyes and hoisted off her horn-rimmed reading glasses from her pixieish face.

Nope. The readers of the Maxville High *Trumpet* wouldn't have a clue to whom Handsome Joe was taking to the Halloween Hop, and it would drive certain parties to absolute distraction.

Diane drained the last of her Diet Pepsi and tossed the empty into the recycling basket with a loud rolling clank of metal meeting metal. She tucked her blue silk blouse back inside the top of her prewashed Levi jeans. Diane was no fashion plate but she liked to dress nicely, if casually, for school. Her smile got even bigger as she chuckled at her private joke. No, the readers of her gossip column "Dying to Know" wouldn't find out, either, because Diane had made a deal with Joe not to ask anyone until later in the week—and then tell only her!

And it only cost an ice cream soda at Brunkhorst's Ice Cream Shoppe.

As Diane turned back to her computer to print out her latest journalistic masterpiece, she had exactly three seconds to feel smug and self-satisfied before the rest of the day was totally ruined. And it was none other than the Evil Sisters who trashed it.

They came into the school newspaper office like rejected actresses from a production of Macbeth. Diane half expected the first words from their mouths to be "Bubble bubble, toil and trouble."

Toni Ayers was first, then Lynn Rivers, and finally Melissa Birch, wielding purses or book bags like weapons.

In Melissa's hand was a folded-up copy of the Maxville High *Trumpet* and on her face was a scowl as black as a thundercloud.

"Delany," she said, slapping the *Trumpet* down on the countertop. "You're dead meat!"

"Is that a threat?" asked Diane, keeping her cool even though Melissa was a good deal taller than she. "Or did I get lost in a Friday the Thirteenth movie and you're Jason without the mask?"

Melissa just kind of goggled at that. She was a big girl but not fat and had the fashion sense to blend colors and shapes to make her look an absolute knockout to boys even though she was almost as tall as they—a big minus in the courtship scene. She had long blonde hair, sculpted in a do that spelled expensive beauty-parlor.

"Is that mouth registered with the police department?" Toni Ayers wanted to know. The lithe, brunette coolly sauntered into the office as if she owned the place. Toni was the brains of the Sisters. She moved with the grace of a dancer and the cunning of a leopard. She wore a green crew neck sweater today, complementing a pleated black skirt and penny loafers. This preppie look perfectly suited her cold dark eyes that looked back now for reinforcement from the third and final Sister, Lynn Rivers.

Lynn, a svelte and pretty brunette, said nothing. She just stood looking sort of uncomfortable and nervous, as if she were trying to remember if she'd left her curling iron on.

They weren't really sisters, of course. "Evil Sisters" was just Diane's name for their clique. She called them evil because of the gossip they spread.

When Diane's boyfriend, Adam Grant, first heard this assessment of the trio, he'd laughed. "Hey, isn't that kinda like the pot calling the kettle black? What do you think you do in that column of yours?"

But Adam eventually came to understand, as soon as he read more of "Dying to Know." Her column was the most popular part of the *Trumpet,* partly because she kept things sweet, witty, and charming, and partly because she got great material. People constantly brought her juicy tidbits about their friends and rivals. Diane did her best to double-check her items, but sometimes errors crept into her column. Still, by keeping things light and frothy—and vague, when the info was questionable—there was never any real damage done.

When it came to dishing dirt, Diane was a rank amateur compared to the Sisters. These girls had been a trio since kindergarten. Throughout their careers in elementary, junior high, and high school they'd hung out together exclusively. Occasionally they'd let an outsider into the group, then just as capriciously snub her.

And it was not done nicely. They were out to hurt.

I found that out all too quickly, thought Diane.

"You want to see my license?" she said now, trying to hide the fact that these girls still unnerved her. "What's the problem?"

Melissa unfolded the paper and gave a dramatic reading of Diane's latest column. By the time she reached the line about "the droppings from my gossip canary"—a line Diane was particularly fond of, she reflected—Melissa's voice was almost shaking with anger. She pinned Diane with a glare. "Really, Diane. We don't need this kind of press."

Diane shrugged. "I don't see anything in there about Lynn, Melissa, or Toni—"

"Oh, come on, Diane!" snapped Toni. "The number three comes up at Maxville, and people think about us. After all, we're the most popular and famous girls in the whole school! Have been since the Dark Ages!"

"Nope. Back then, they would have burned you at the stake."

Melissa Birch lurched at Diane, but Lynn grabbed her shoulder, restraining her. "Not here, not now. Remember, Melissa. We're ladies." She turned her attention back to Diane. "Look, Delany, I guess when you came here last year we had a little . . . misunderstanding."

"I'll say!" said Diane. "You gave me some false information for this column! Information that hurt people. 'Dying to Know' is for fun, not for your personal gratification."

"As I said, Diane, a misunderstanding. We've forgiven you"—Lynn smiled slyly, looking like Winona Ryder with a funny secret. "But apparently you haven't forgiven us. So now, why don't we just bury the hatchet—"

"In her head!" said Melissa.

"Excuse my friend. She watches too much TV." Toni tried on a sweet, disarming smile. It fit surprisingly well. "Now then, Diane, about that unfortunate business of Rick Elkins." She turned to her colleagues. "Maybe you're right in the column. Maybe Melissa and Lynn got a little too . . . imaginative when they mentioned Rick."

"Us?" said Lynn. "Toni, it was you who—"

A sudden glare, cold as the last Ice Age, cut her short. Then the smile beamed back, and Toni's voice was soft and reasonable.

"Anyway, Diane, they're very sorry about the little—slipups concerning Rick. I've personally apologized to Rick—so now we thought maybe you might want to include that little news item in your next column."

Diane wasn't sure that an apology was enough after what the Sisters had done to Rick. He'd been doing so well before the rumors started, and now he was even talking about not going out for baseball in the spring.

"Oh, right. You help put the guy back into deep depression and you think a little 'I'm sorry' can change everything?"

"Look, can I help it if the guy has a lousy past and a rotten home life?" said Toni.

"No, but you can keep your mouth shut once in a while!"

Toni let that pass. "What's over is over, Diane,"

she said, that cold smile fixed on her face. She tapped the paper with a long bright red fingernail. "Hard cold print is a little more difficult to deal with." She took a deep breath and thoughtfully scratched her nose. "Look, Diane, I realize that we started off on the wrong foot."

"Oh, we started off on the right foot—it was the wrong foot that came later!" said Diane.

Diane's troubles with Lynn, Melissa, and Toni had started the year before when she had first moved to Maxville. Having some journalistic experience at her previous school, she had decided that a gossip column would be a great way to meet people. And lo and behold, the *Trumpet* editors were looking for just such a writer.

Unfortunately, Diane hadn't known very many people then. The first folks who had knocked on her door had been the Evil Sisters. Alas, she hadn't known about the "evil" part then. All she'd seen was the most glamorous and exclusive trio in school, actually wanting to be friends. They'd taken her into their "little clan" as they called it, making sure that she sat with them at lunch and got all the same percs they did, as popular girls at school. They also nattered on incessantly about this or that person they knew, making sure that Diane got all the hints and news they dropped.

Naturally, she used it in her fledgling column, and when the Sisters saw items that they'd given her, they seemed especially pleased.

It all seemed—well, too good to be true.

As it turned out, it was.

About a month after she started using these tidbits that the Sisters dropped her, the truth gradually began to filter down to her: the information that Lynn, Melissa, and Toni had fed her was false. From teachers and students, she'd learned that they'd already earned quite a reputation as not just gossip mongers—but malicious gossip mongers, who spread rumors specifically to hurt people who had slighted them, or to whom they had taken a dislike.

They had been using her to barbecue their latest victims, and she hadn't been aware of this.

First, she had personally sought out those victims and apologized to them. Then, in a particularly long column, she had not only publicly acknowledged her previous "factual" errors, but mercilessly parodied the years-long reign of the Evil Sisters hilariously and in good spirits. She'd personally confronted them with a copy of the paper itself, and then explained why she had done what she'd done.

Diane hadn't expected them to take it well—but hadn't expected the reaction she'd gotten.

They'd totally shut her out. Cold-shoulder time. Not only that, she began to hear all sorts of nasty rumors about herself.

War!

So this had continued for a full year now—with snipes and shots exchanged at school games, in the Maxville High gym, and near hall lockers—and especially at lunchtime, when gab was at absolute high ebb.

But there hadn't been a real confrontation—until now.

"So anyway, Diane," said Toni, "I sincerely hope that we can call a truce to this whole business." She picked the *Trumpet* up again, glanced at the column, and clucked her tongue sadly. "I guess maybe

31

we kinda blew it, giving you all that wrong info. But you know, all that stuff—well, it was from our point of view. And I guess you know when you've got different people involved, you've got different versions of things.''

"That may be true, but your version is more malicious and mean-spirited than most.''

Toni put on a hurt expression. "We don't think we're malicious or mean-spirited. Maybe you see us this way because we've been having a bit of a . . . well, no, Not a bit . . . it's an out-and-out feud.''

"Right,'' said Melissa, her glare burning again. "Bring out the guns!''

"Melissa! I wish you wouldn't be so violent!'' said Lynn, who had kept to the rear of the other girls, but took this opportunity to speak up. Melissa gave her a dirty look. Diane sensed that the two had been arguing earlier.

Toni just ignored the squabble, returning to the subject at hand. "And this feud is not doing us any good, and it certainly isn't doing you any good!''

"Oh, I don't know about that,'' piped Diane perkily. "It makes for good copy!''

The Evil Sisters took a slow burn on that one, but Toni put up her hand to halt any outburst. "What do you want? We're certainly not going to beg.''

Diane was a little bit astonished. The Sisters seemed to be willing to make some kind of deal. She couldn't pass up this kind of opportunity!

"Okay,'' she said. She'd always hoped this kind of thing would happen, and she knew just what to say. "I'll tell you what. I won't mention you anymore—or the rotten things you do and say—on one condition.''

"What's that?" said Melissa, taking the bait.

"You guys calm down. Stop hurting people. Gossip is one thing, but you three go too far. Cut it out, and I promise I'll never talk about the Evil Sisters again. But only as long as I never hear again that you've made someone's life miserable."

"We don't mean to—" said Lynn.

"Quiet," said Toni sharply. "Deal." Her petite hand shot out to seal the bargain. Diane found herself shaking hands and looking at Toni's smile. "Maybe we have been a little too rough on people. We'll take it easier. . . . Please, though, we don't need this kind of press anymore."

"All right," said Diane, wondering if this was the way it felt to make a deal with the devil. "Just remember, I don't want to hear any more about ruined lives due to your wagging tongues!"

Toni gestured, a sly smile on her face. "Cross our hearts," she said.

"And hope to die," said Lynn, looking troubled.

BEFORE

FIONA MACKENSIE

Fiona MacKensie was excited.

As she sat in the foyer of the Holiday Inn, she felt very excited indeed, more excited than she'd felt in her entire life!

The future looked very rosy, but at this time, at this moment, all she could think about was *now*.

The seventeen year old couldn't help fidgeting a bit in her chair as she waited. She hardly noticed the bustle of people through the lobby. People checking out, people checking in. All she could see now was Mr. Hughes up at the front desk, talking to the attendants.

He looked so tall and strong and handsome, even from the back. She'd always thought Mr. Hughes was handsome, even before she'd been in his class. But now . . . now that he'd paid so much attention to her this year, now that he called her Fi and she called him Ken, instead of Mr. Hughes, she felt so *close* to him. Close enough to allow him to take her here to the Holiday Inn, to do this. Close enough to put *everything* in his hands.

Mr. Hughes . . . no, *Ken*, finished at the reception

desk. He walked back to her, smiling, his eyes flashing with that special sexy glint that intelligent handsome men have. As he looked at her, Fiona saw nothing but a reflection of her own excitement, admiration . . . and yes, affection.

"Okay. All set. Room 2113."

"Okay!"

He sat down on the chair across from her, reached out and collected her hand in his.

"Are you nervous?"

"Uhm." She giggled and looked around. She realized that they were in the lobby of a hotel, and that *anybody* might walk in and see them. "Well, yeah, I guess so."

"That's okay. You know, experienced as I am in this sort of thing, I guess I'm sort of nervous myself."

"You are? Why?"

"You've come to mean a lot to me, I guess, Fiona."

Her heart seemed to skip a beat. If she'd had any doubt before about what she was doing at this hotel with Ken Hughes, Maxville High School English lit teacher, it was extinguished by that one sentence.

He squeezed her hand reassuringly. "C'mon, then. Let's go."

"Yes. Let's do it!"

She got up, and they started walking toward the elevators.

Part of the lobby consisted of a few businesses, including a miniversion of the local drugstore chain, Star Pharmacies. As they walked past, Fiona glimpsed one of the patrons inside.

Oh God. Not *her!*

"Uhm, Mr. Hughes . . . Ken," she said. "Maybe we could take the stairs. I'm feeling a little nervous still, and maybe the exercise would help."

"No problem!" He guided her quickly through the hallway, which was good, because they didn't have to linger, waiting for the elevator.

Which was good, because if they stuck around too long, for sure Melissa Birch, gossip extraordinaire, would see them. She'd tell her compatriot witches, and well, it would snowball from there.

And that would spell trouble, *big* trouble for both of them.

But by the time they got all the way up to the second floor, and Ken Hughes's strong and reassuring presence had comforted her and renewed her excitement, Fiona wasn't thinking about Melissa Birch, or her Evil Sisters.

Not at all.

She had never done it before, but she performed well. As though she'd been doing this kind of thing all her life!

Afterwards Fiona felt good.

No, she felt *great!*

As they left the hotel room, Ken Hughes couldn't help leaning over to hug her.

"Fiona! You were wonderful!!" said Mr. Hughes.

And she knew she had been.

"Thanks, Mr. Hughes . . . I mean, Ken. I couldn't have done it without you."

"Well, I don't know about that. I just set it up for you," he said as they walked along the hall, back to the stairs they had climbed to get there. "You were the one who pulled the grades and the SATs.

You were the one who did so well on the interview. Princeton . . . that's the one you think you're going to go with?''

"That's the one you recommended!''

"Well, after your interview with that scout, I should think that you could pretty much have your choice of schools!'' His eyes shone fondly. "I was really proud of you in there, Fiona. You were articulate, self-possessed, poised—and you even kept your extraordinary sense of humor. You had old Haggerty eating out of your hand.''

"I guess he did want to have dinner with us, didn't he?'' she said, laughing. "But that wouldn't do at all. I mean, if my parents found out that I'm here interviewing for a school so far away from their dear old alma mater—''

"Duke is a fine school, Fiona. There's no question you could go there. You can have your pick, but there's absolutely no reason why your education wouldn't be splendid at Duke University!''

"I told you, Mr. Hughes,'' she said, a little less warmly, a little more assertively. "No *way* am I going *there!* I'm my own person. I have to forge my own path. I don't need my parents' money. I'm going to get scholarships, so I can choose the college that *I* want to go to. My acceptance at Duke was pretty much assured—but I had to reach out further on my own.'' She took a deep breath. "But having you for that special course this summer and then for English lit this year has done absolute wonders for my self-confidence. Thanks, Ken. Thanks so much.'' She couldn't help herself. She kissed him.

It was just a peck on the cheek, but Mr. Hughes got quite red and embarrassed and pulled away from her embrace. "That's very sweet of you, Fi. But you know, you could have done it on your own. I just faciliated the interview, that's all."

"No. I'll never believe that. And I just hope, Mr. Hughes," she said, getting a little more formal, realizing that yes, she *did* have just an eensy weensy crush on the guy, and she should be a little more reserved in her behavior. "I just hope that we can *always* be friends."

He looked much more comfortable with that, smiling, showing his even white teeth. "I'm sure of that, Fi. I'm very sure."

They were back down the steps and into the lobby, analyzing the interview, when Fiona had the distinct feeling that someone was watching them.

She turned around, and her stomach did an immediate flip-flop.

There, standing in the lobby, leaning against the wall, was Melissa Birch. There was a definite malicious look in the girl's eye. She made a "Naughty, naughty!" gesture, smiled, and then strode away in the opposite direction.

Mr. Hughes didn't even notice Melissa, but he did notice Fiona's reaction. ". . . and so then I thought . . . Say . . . are you okay, Fi? You look like someone just walked over your grave."

She shook it off. Nah. There was no harm. There was no proof of anything. "I just hope somebody's not *digging* my grave."

"Pardon?"

"Nothing. So what were you saying, Mr. Hughes?"

He continued. And as he walked her back out to her car, Fiona MacKensie thought, it had better be nothing. It better not get back to my parents that I was on this interview, and if it does, I'll know that one of those three witches are responsible. Melissa Birch, Toni Ayers, Lynn Rivers.

And if it did . . . if they ruined this for her . . .

She'd *kill* them!

One by one, she'd *kill* them!

1

On the evening that changed her entire life, Diane Delany had a feeling, a *bad* feeling like a stomach-ache that wouldn't go away. It was this feeling that took her to a realization that she couldn't ignore.

She had to go talk to the girl.

I've really got to have a good heart-to-heart with Lynn Rivers. This thought echoed over and over in her mind as Diane drove to Lynn's house.

If there was one member of the Evil Sisters who had a hope of redemption, it was Lynn. *I can be quite cynical,* Diane thought as she pulled the car into the Rivers's driveway, *but I definitely believe that everyone has good qualities if you look hard enough. Sheesh, maybe even Melissa and Toni. But Melissa and Toni I don't think I can talk to now. Maybe I can with Lynn.*

She climbed the stairs of the Rivers's house.

Although most of the house was dark, Lynn's bedroom light was on.

She was home all right.

It seemed to have gotten colder and darker. Diane zipped up her jacket, but she still felt a little shivery.

I've got to make Lynn understand the harm that she and her friends are doing.

This last batch of rumors was just the last straw!

After their confrontation over the Rick Elkins incident, she thought maybe the Evil Sisters had seen the light. But now it was starting up again.

Lynn seemed like her only hope. When Diane had heard rumors and innuendo about Fiona MacKensie, she'd made a pointed reference to the story in Lynn's presence in the girl's locker room.

A glimmer of fear, of vulnerability, despite the protestations of innocence, of loyalty to the other girls. That had been the clincher.

Her intuition told her that Lynn would be the one to talk to.

A breeze blew, skirting the old wood of the porch, tinkling the wind chimes that hung there like an earring dangling from an old wooden ear. Everything felt empty, curiously desolate, and with the sun gone now and hardly any light, it was all . . . well, rather *spooky*.

Diane went up and knocked on the door.

It creaked open at the pressure of her fist, and her knocks echoed hollowly through the house.

She rapped emphatically on the doorjamb. "Hello!" she said. "Is anybody there?"

There was no answer.

However, Diane realized, there *was* sound coming from someplace. It was music—heavy metal music— played at a low volume.

"Hello!" she said. "It's Diane Delany!"

Still no answer.

Normally Diane would have just gone away. After all, even though she knew the family, entering a

41

house was not only trespassing. It was also being *nosy* and what with her reputation as gossip columnist for the *Trumpet*, she didn't need any bad raps about breaking into people's houses, digging for dirt.

But Diane had the distinct feeling that something was *wrong* here. *Very* wrong.

The house had that awful something-bad-has-happened-here feel, as if it were holding its breath. There was the smell of bacon from the morning's breakfast in the air, but nothing else. There was an empty feel to the place as well, even though the door was open, music was playing, and there were lights on in a couple of rooms.

"Hello? Lynn? Nadine? Mr. and Mrs. Rivers?"

Absolutely no response, and Diane felt obliged to investigate. She stepped through the doorway and hesitantly walked through the shadows of the living room, still hearing no sounds except the music. A light flowed down the staircase from the second story, so Diane decided that she'd check upstairs first.

"It's me—Diane," she said several times, like a litany of explanation for her intrusion. "Diane Delany."

It was an old house, filled with lots of antique furniture—unfortunately, the steps were old too. Despite the thick carpeting, the steps *creaked* under her feet. All this boosted the general creepy feeling of the whole adventure. Halfway up, she wished she'd never come in, never even come here. . . .

But now that she was inside, she might as well find out if everything was okay. If something *was* wrong, the Rivers family would probably appreciate the thought if not the intrusion. . . .

At the landing, the floorboards stopped creaking. Diane peered down the hallway. Lights were on in what she knew to be Lynn's bedroom and in the family bathroom.

She'd check the bedroom first.

Upstairs the house had a pleasant cedar and lavender smell and the familiarity of the scent was a comfort. Lynn's door was half open. Diane went in, hoping to see Lynn stretched out on the bed wearing her stereo headphones.

No such luck.

The bed was neatly made and empty. On the other side of the room was Lynn's dresser and a desk. Although there was a typewriter on the desk and a copy of Slyvia Plath's *The Bell Jar* and a volume of her poems, there was no evidence that Lynn had been working on her English paper.

Diane's natural curiosity almost made her take a closer look around the neat room for possible evidence of other Evil Sisters' foul deeds, but she stopped herself. That would be beyond the boundaries of decency, she knew.

Besides, she had the bathroom to check.

The bathroom door was half open.

Water was trickling across the sill, staining the carpeting in the hall darkly.

"Hello?" she said. She felt particularly funny invading the bathroom, and it was unlikely that Lynn would be listening to her headphones in there anyway. Most likely, the place was empty and so was the whole house and what she should do was just go back down to the front door, write a note, see if there was a way to lock the front door from the inside, and then leave.

Just one peek inside the bathroom first, though, just to be complete.

Although it was an old bathroom, and it was certainly the *biggest* that Diane had ever seen, it was still a modern American family's bathroom, complete with towels and toothbrushes, hair dryers, mirrors, tile, toilet, sink, and the usual plethora of soaps, shampoos, and ointments. The air was damp as if a shower had been taken recently, and Diane's eyes naturally gravitated toward the huge old-fashioned bathtub with ceramic and stainless steel taps.

Lynn Rivers lay in the bathtub.

Her head was resting in one of those inflatable cushions on the edge. Her eyes were closed. Diane thought she must be asleep.

"Lynn?"

Funny though, the way her head lolled . . .

Diane stepped forward, and that was when she saw the image she would never be able to erase from her mind.

The water of the tub, filled to the brim, was colored a deep crimson. In the soap dish on the side was a bloody straight razor.

Stunned, unable to take in what was before her eyes, Diane stood there for a long moment. Then, as though in a some dreadful waking dream, she stepped forward.

"Lynn," she whispered.

The girl's arms were submerged in the darkly stained water, but her pale neck was exposed enough to take a pulse.

Diane hesitantly touched it.

She gasped and stepped back.

Not only did Lynn Rivers not have a pulse, she was getting *cold*.

Lynn Rivers was dead.

For several more moments Diane could only stare down at the body in the bathtub. Then she had to look away. A horrible realization turned her insides to ice.

Suicide . . .

Lynn Rivers had *killed* herself.

At first, she felt the urge to just turn, run down the stairs and *out* of this old house and hide.

Do it! said a voice inside her head. *Just run away! No one will ever know you've even been here! There's absolutely no proof.*

But even as she started to move away, she knew that she could never live with herself if she did *that*.

No, she had to face up to the truth.

She'd found the body of Lynn Rivers, a suicide, and had to deal with reporting it. Taking in a slow and steady series of breaths, Diane went to call the police.

DYING TO KNOW

a column by
Diane Delany

    Due to recent tragic events, there will be no column this week.

DYING TO KNOW

a column by
Diane Delany
(unpublished)

Dear Curious Reader!

You'll just have to keep on *being* curious, won't you, because you're never going to read this.

I read somewhere that writing things out helps relieve trauma. Well, after what happened this evening I just can't seem to go to sleep. So I'm at my desk now, writing it out.

Sigh.

I wish Lynn would have asked for help. I would have done anything, *anything* to help her!

But, realizing that I had no power over the situation, I can't help having another, more selfish wish.

I wish I hadn't been the one ...

The one to find Lynn like that ...

I mean, I *shouldn't* have been the one! It was just the way events worked out, me wanting to talk to her and all. Adam always says I get *too* involved in these things, and I can't disagree with him now, feeling the way I do, unable to forget that bloody body in the tub....

No. Don't think about it. Get it out of your mind, kiddo. Write about something else. Yeah, write about *Adam!*

Now there's a subject, dear reader! Oh, if you only knew the truth, *that* would be the *sex* scandal of Maxville. Or rather *negative* sex scandal. Adam wants to, and I'm holding out. It's a girl's prerogative, right? Still, he never lets me forget how amorous and physical he is. Like one day in the library, I'm studying and he comes up and fondles me! I mean, right out in *public!* If anyone had *seen!* That was the day he told me about his friend Jim Stevens, the guy with the former klepto problem that got leaked by the Evil Sisters. On one hand Adam can be so infuriating it's incredible—and then, he'll be concerned and caring about a friend! I don't know.... He's such a Jekyll and Hyde character, he scares me sometimes.

Anyway, that was when I first knew that the Sisters were still up to no good *even though* I'd warned them to lay off the dirt!

The final straw was when I heard the rumor about Fiona MacKensie and Mr. Hughes! I ran into Fiona out in front of the school, waiting for a ride. She was talking with Heather Perkins, another Sisters' victim. I heard her side of the story, about actually going to the Holiday Inn for an interview with a college scout and it made a lot of sense. More sense than the vicious rumors the Evil Sisters were spreading. After they'd made a deal with me to lay off.

And *that*, nosy reader, is why I took it upon myself to go and talk to Lynn Rivers. Lynn and I used to be friends, and I figured I might be able to talk to her. You know, either get her to convince the others to stop the harm they were doing ... or to get out. I'd tried that earlier, talking to her in the girls' locker room.

"Why do you hang out with those witches?" I asked her.

"They're my friends," she'd said. "They're closer than ... than *family*. I mean, we've been through *everything!*"

Yeah. Like through every clothing catalog!

"I always thought that you had hope, Lynn. That you just went along with the things they wanted you to do."

She just blathered more about being so close, such good friends with Toni and Melissa.

"Don't you see it, Lynn? They're just *using* you!"

But it wouldn't work then. She said something nasty about "Dying to Know" and called me Miss Buttinsky and stormed off.

I don't know *why* I thought I could talk to her today.

But I knew that I had to *try*.

The thing is, dear unaware reader, the really painful thing, is that I *really care* about you. I really care about my high school. I want it to be a *really cool place*. And it can't be a cool place when people like the Evil Sisters do what they do to other people!

Sigh.

I wish Adam were here now, to hold me.

No, maybe I don't. I don't know if I could really trust him. Maybe he'd just use the opportunity to try to get amorous while I was weak.

I wish I had never gone to Lynn Rivers's house.

But then, I did.

And I'm going to have to learn to live with what I saw, even though it'll change my life.

There. I don't know if I feel better, but it's written.

Now I'm going to tear this up so nobody reads it, and try to get some sleep.

2

She felt empty. Sad and empty.

"Hi, honey," said her father. "Is there anything I can get you?"

It was Monday afternoon. Diane lay on her bed in her darkened room holding Buttons, an old teddy bear. Her room was a mess, but it had the familiar smell of her clothes and perfume that always comforted her when she was upset. She still wore the black coat and pants she'd worn earlier in the day to the police inquiry into Lynn Rivers's death. But she'd kicked off the black flats. She'd thought about putting some music on the radio, but just didn't have the energy to do anything. She just felt terribly, terribly *empty*.

"No thanks, Dad. I'm fine."

"I think your mom made some tea. She's going to be up in a moment with it," continued her father, entering. He sat down at the end of the bed as he usually did and put a comforting but respectful hand on her shoulder. "How are you doing, kitten? I mean, really."

Diane sighed. Her father's concern was great. She

loved him. And although he did get stuffy sometimes and did the "daddy dance" pretty much the same way most of her friends' fathers did, he had a kind of understanding that most other fathers seemed to lack. Nonetheless, right now all she really wanted was to be left alone to go through whatever she had to go through on her own.

"I'm okay. Really I am, Dad."

"That was pretty rough, what you had to do. I mean, dealing with the police is no treat at the best of times—but on this kind of matter . . . And after what happened last night. I must say, Diane, I guess you're a lot more mature than I gave you credit for. You handled it all very well. I'm very, very proud of you."

"Thanks, Dad." His male presence was very much with her; she could smell his usual Old Spice aftershave very strongly, along with the peculiar blend of paper and pencils and wood that had made her feel very safe and secure at frightening times as a child. He seemed a lot smaller now than then, a lot less strong and commanding. Now she realized that he was just a normal-sized man. Still, he was very special. Usually, when she was upset, she would just let go and reach to him for a warm and cozy hug. But now, she just felt listless and apathetic.

Her father talked to her gently, a little about what he had planned for the holidays, just trying to be there for her. But Diane spaced out, morbidly flashing back to Sunday evening back at the Rivers house and what had happened right after she'd found Lynn's body.

The phone. The harsh cop voice. The lights . . . the red lights . . .

She'd called 911, of course. Pretty soon there were red lights twirling all over the place. The sheriff came after the rescue team and asked her questions.

The dull anxiety, dread, horror. . .

The grief.

That had been tough, but comparatively easier than facing the Rivers family. A neighbor attracted by the commotion knew that the rest of the family was visiting relatives about sixty miles away. Lynn had stayed home to finish an English paper. Whether or not working on a term paper on a famous poet-suicide had driven her to emulate the artist was not known. No suicide note was found. Everyone seemed to accept Diane's account of why she'd entered the house. But witnessing the Rivers family's grief firsthand had been pretty rugged. As she'd confided to Adam this morning on the phone, she'd been forced to grow up about ten years in two hours.

Now she felt all used up. She just wanted to vegetate.

But her father seemed to think something more was needed.

"Ah. Here's your mother."

He stood up and went to the door, opening it for his wife. April Delany, her graying hair looking uncharacteristically mussed, carried in the best silver service on a tray and put it on the dresser. "I thought you'd like a cup of tea, dear. Earl Grey, your favorite."

"Thanks, Mom."

"And some of your favorite cookies. Lorna Doones."

"Great."

"Do you want me to pour it for you and put the milk and sugar in it?"

"Okay."

"Here you go, dear."

"Just put it on the table, Mom."

Her mother studied her for a moment. "I'm sorry all this happened, dear. You know I am. But I can't help saying that I could have predicted that something bad would come from all this gossip column business."

"April," said Mr. Delany, "do you really think that now's the time?"

"That's okay, Dad. She's going to do it sooner or later. It might as well be now."

"Well, don't you think I have a point, dear?" said Mrs. Delany, trying to sound sweet but instead just sounding controlled.

"What do you want me to do? Stop writing the column?"

"I think you should consider that, yes."

"I don't see what this has to do with my column."

"Perhaps you should think about that, too."

"Dad, I really appreciate your concern. And, Mom, thanks so much for your advice. But you know, I really didn't want any of this to happen. I'm not feeling so good right now—so could you just leave me alone for a while? Please?" Diane turned away from them so she didn't have to look at them.

"But, Diane," said her mother, "we only want what's best for you!"

"Come on, April. Let her have this time. You can lecture her later."

"I'm sorry, dear. You will drink your tea, won't you."

"Yeah, Mom."

They left quietly. Diane lay there for a few minutes, not moving a muscle. Then she thought that maybe that cup of tea might at least make her feel something.

She took a sip, and she remembered a time back when she had just come to Maxville and hadn't known anybody, and Lynn Rivers had been so sweet and kind to her. She had visited Lynn and they had sipped Earl Grey tea together, and Lynn had told her some of the Maxville High gossip. Diane had thought that Lynn was just the most wonderful person then.

Thinking of all that had happened since that innocent day, she put the cup of tea back down into the saucer and she began to sob softly into her pillow.

The terrible sadness!

"I'm very sorry about . . . about all this," said Diane to Nadine Rivers. The last strains of the organ music for Lynn's memorial service at the Maxville Community Center had just died away. The sick-sweet smell of funeral flowers hung in the air. *I feel as black as my dress.* She stood by Adam Grant now, holding on to his arm as though she was afraid that if she didn't, she'd fall down.

Nadine nodded. "Hi, Diane. Thanks. This is my older brother, Patrick, down from the seminary."

"This is my friend, Adam Grant." She looked up at Adam. Having him here made her feel better. Adam Grant was a trifle under six feet tall, but his large square shoulders and slender hips made him look taller. He had sandy hair but dark eyes, an arresting combination. Usually his eyes sparkled with a lively, sexy mischief and his hands were animated, often in ways Diane found distracting, sometimes more distracting than she liked. But today his eyes were steady and grim, his hands were still and respectful.

"Yes. I've met Adam," said Nadine, giving him a look that was hard to read. But before Diane could think about much of anything else, Patrick was busy shaking their hands and, like the minister-in-training he was, calming them with soft, comforting words.

"Such a beautiful service, don't you think?" said the darkly handsome young man. "It's so reassuring that in these modern days, a community can pull together at such a sad time."

A wise move, too, thought Diane. She'd read about suicides at high schools. One often triggered another. Doubtless the authorities thought that a memorial service—along with a speech concerning counseling services available—might save some lives.

Adam, a bit tongue-tied, could only nod and look uncomfortable.

"I'm going to miss Lynn," said Diane. "But most of all I wish there was some way of letting you two know that your sister's life . . . well, it meant something to me, I guess."

Nadine looked at her in a funny way. "Thanks."

"We appreciate that," said Patrick, his voice cracking a bit. "We truly do. Now, if you'll excuse us, there are a few things we have to attend to. And then I have to get my sister home. These past few days have been very trying."

True. Too true.

"Just a moment, Pat." Nadine stepped over and

whispered in Diane's ear, "I'll be seeing you soon, Diane."

She stepped back, shot an unreadable look at Adam, and was gone.

"What was that all about?" said Adam.

"She said she'd be seeing me soon. Do you two know each other from before?"

"Oh . . . yeah. I . . . uh . . . did some work for her father and we met then. Strange girl, huh?"

Diane sighed and tried to let the whole thing go. "I just think right now, Adam, that I'd like to go home."

Her heart gave a lurch.

There they were, coming toward her. Diane didn't know how she was going to deal with them. The Evil Sisters. Minus Lynn Rivers.

"Diane?" said Toni in a subdued voice. "Okay if we sit with you?"

"Yeah. We need to talk," added Melissa in almost a whisper.

They placed their trays of salad and low-fat milk on the table. *They certainly look mournful enough*. Toni and Melissa both wore black blouses and black designer Guess? jeans. The only color in these ensembles were red scarves. The effect, thought Diane, was more Edward Gorey than anything else, but apparently the rest of the school found their look sufficiently chastened and grieving.

"We realize we've been wrong, terribly wrong," said Toni, eyes downcast. "We want to apologize to you, Diane, for going back on our word."

"And we want the record to show," continued

Melissa, "that no longer will we cast asp . . . asper—"

"Aspersions," said Toni in a clipped, annoyed voice.

"Aspersions," parroted Melissa, keeping the sad frown plastered on her face.

Was it a mask?

It seemed real enough. And it was understandable that Lynn's death would make the remaining Sisters reconsider their ways. She had been their buddy for simply *ages*—and now she was gone.

It was a time for soul searching among all the Maxville High School students. Although they'd all heard about the teen suicide problem sweeping the nation, this was the first time in anyone's memory that something like this had happened. The fact that the person who had killed herself was one of the school's most popular students, a girl from a comfortable background with no history of mental imbalance, was all the more startling.

It meant that this peculiar teenage disease had touched Maxville—and that meant it could strike again.

After the news had spread like wildfire the next day, Dr. Morgan, Maxville's principal, had called an assembly at which a local psychologist spoke on the subject of teen suicide. Free counseling was offered to anyone who felt the need.

Many Maxville students were availing themselves of this service. Although Maxville still grieved, even the victims of the Three Sisters' tongues, the school administration felt that at least Lynn Rivers's suicide might indirectly help other troubled students.

"I'm happy to hear that." Yes, she was! "I don't

know if I'm going to be continuing my column though."

Toni Ayers blinked. "But you've got to!"

"Why? I can't help feeling that if this little war of ours contributed in any way to Lynn's decision . . . well, then I've done a great deal of harm."

"That's nonsense. Isn't it, Melissa?"

"Hmmmm? Oh, yeah. Nonsense!" Her brows knitted. "Uhmm . . . Why is it, uh, nonsense, Toni?"

"It's nonsense because the way Lynn was headed had nothing to do with 'Dying to Know' or anything else. She was seriously depressed. Wasn't she, Melissa?"

Melissa sighed as though the weight of the world were on her shoulders. "Very depressed. We tried to cheer her up all the time, and I guess maybe she did get happier when she was around us . . . which was why we didn't see all this coming. But we were away that weekend, and so we couldn't help her. But yeah, I don't know what it was, chemical or the music she listened to . . . but Lynn was one depressed camper. . . . Although clearly much more depressed than we thought or, goodness knows, we would have made sure that she got *professional* help." She looked over at Toni as if for approval.

Toni, wearing no makeup and looking wilted and beaten, nodded. "That's right. So Melissa and I have examined ourselves very closely and decided that perhaps we weren't exactly being as nice to other students as we might be. You have to understand that having so many advantages and so—well, just being so generally *superior* to other students has always made us look down on them. We realize that maybe this has been a mistake. So, I guess, Diane, you could say that Melissa and I . . . are re-forming.''

"No more gossip?" She had heard *that* one before. Could she believe them this time?

Toni's mouth twitched a bit, as though she were a smoker who'd just sworn off cigarettes. "We will try to say only nice things about other people.''

Diane examined her former adversaries. They *seemed* sincere. She nodded. "Okay. It's a deal. Tell you what. We can all gossip. I mean, it's human. But only fun stuff, okay?''

"You mean you're going to keep 'Dying to Know'?''

"I'll consider it.''

"Excellent!'' said Melissa.

Toni scowled at her friend. "What Melissa means is that it would make us feel very, very bad to think that we contributed to the demise of such a vital part of the school community life.''

Toni attended to her salad, her expression still very serious.

However, Melissa started to prattle on about the latest winter fashion that she'd seen last night at the mall.

Diane spaced out, her thoughts again returning, as they seemed to do so often, to the scene at the Rivers's house Sunday night. *The dead body adrift in the bathtub. The blood. The strange smell: soap, water, sweet-sick copper*. These nightmares would cling for a long, long time.

"Can you quote us in your column, Diane?'' said Toni. "Can you give us a chance to say some nice things about Lynn for the record?''

Diane blinked. Sure. Why not? "Just write something down, and if it seems right, I'll use it."

"Fair enough," said Toni, uncharacteristically agreeable. "We miss Lynn, Diane. We really do. And we're really sincere about this. Of course, we still want Maxville High to look up to us as special—but we also want to hold the memory of Lynn Rivers in our hearts and our behavior."

"I understand," said Diane.

We'll wait and see.

Even with the shock they'd undoubtedly suffered, Diane still wasn't sure the remaining Evil Sisters could be so quickly and completely reformed.

3

"Diane, I need to talk to you. It's urgent."

Sheesh! Like I really need to be interrupted!

Diane looked up from her history book, feeling annoyed. That test on Franklin Roosevelt's New Deal in seventh period American history class today was going to be a killer, and she'd hardly done any studying. This happened all the time, people coming up to her while she was occupied with something else, wanting to give her some ridiculous (and often untrue) gossip for her column. She looked up, ready to blow the person off.

"You know, this is study hall and I—"

But when she realized who it was, she stopped mid sentence.

It was Nadine Rivers, Lynn Rivers's younger sister.

"Really, it's very important, Diane, or honest, I wouldn't bother you like this."

Nadine was unusually tall for a freshman. She had long thin hair, blonde just like Lynn's but not as pretty. In fact, Nadine was a skinnier, ganglier version of her sister, a prototypical just-grown-up girl still a bit dizzy from being so high up in the air and not at all adjusted to the business of being a teenager. She was wearing the unofficial school uniform of jeans and a soft blouse, and it was clear that her older sister had given her lessons in what to wear—but she just didn't yet have the poise and presence that her more spectacular sibling had had.

In her hand she grasped a writing tablet as though it were the most important thing in the world.

"This," Nadine announced a little breathlessly, her blue eyes wide, "was the last thing that my sister ever wrote."

She handed it to Diane, who reluctantly took it.

"Oh God," said Diane, looking at it with misgivings.

"Read it."

"No one said anything about a suicide note."

Nadine put her books down on the library desk and sat down, keeping her eyes steadily on Diane. "Just read it. It's very, very important."

Feminine handwriting, all curlicues and cuteness.

It was only a page and a half long, so it read pretty quickly. When she was finished, she looked back up at Nadine Rivers, a little gape mouthed. "I don't get it."

"I was upstate at another school. Month-long exchange thing, you know. Science." Nadine sighed. "Lynn and I were good friends, besides being sisters. She would write me letters because she missed me. And you know, I never really appreciated them." She sighed again. "Now I really miss Lynn . . . and I can't write her letters."

Diane looked again at the letter.

. . . having a great time here . . . you should have been in church today, it was just so pretty with the flowers and the lights through the stained glass windows. . . . And Nadine, the organist played Handel today. Your fave! I like Bach and Mozart better, you know, but today I liked Handel a lot because it reminded me of you. . . . Anyway, things are getting pretty darned interesting. . . .

How odd!

She looked up, certain that her bafflement read on her face.

"Nadine . . . this isn't a suicide note. And the date . . . why it's the day your sister died."

"Exactly. Now does this read like someone who felt so depressed she wanted to kill herself?"

"No. But you never know. . . ."

Nadine shook her head. "Lynn *confided* in me in her letters. This isn't what she would have written if she . . ."

A dread silence crept between them. A shiver went down Diane's spine. "Nadine, why did you come to me. Why are you showing me this letter . . .?"

"Because, I don't think that my sister killed herself," she said in a potent whisper. "I think that someone *murdered her!*"

Murder.

Murder was what you watched on television or read about in mysteries or saw in the paper. It wasn't something that happened to someone you knew.

Hard to grasp the possibility . . .

"Don't you think maybe you're being a little too melodramatic here, Nadine?"

Nadine's expression remained totally serious. "No.

64

No, I don't. I knew my sister too well. Sure, she had problems. I have problems, you have problems, *everyone* has problems. But I know that Lynn didn't have enough problems to want to kill herself.''

"Well, I don't know. . . . She often seemed *troubled* by stuff.''

"She was always that way. But you know, it was really *thoughtful*, not troubled. Lynn thought about stuff. . . . Just a heck of a lot more than those awful girls she ran around with.''

"That's a whole different kettle of curlers.'' Diane took a little time to be thoughtful herself. "Anyway, you still haven't got any kind of proof, right? Just a feeling . . .''

"I know deep down that Lynn didn't kill herself.''

"Okay. So the other question is why me? If you suspect foul play, why are you reporting it to me and not the police, like you should?''

Nadine took the tablet back from Diane's hand. "This—and my gut feeling—is all I have to go on. And I know that's not enough for the police. . . .''

"They didn't find any evidence of foul play.''

"That didn't mean there wasn't any.''

"Okay. But again, why me?''

"Because you're a snoop.''

"Well, thanks.''

"No, I don't mean it in a bad way. . . . What's the term. An 'investigative journalist.' I really think, Diane, that you can help me . . . well, you know . . . investigate this thing. I realize that you don't believe me but . . . but . . .'' Tears suddenly brimmed in her eyes. "I don't know, Diane. . . . If someone killed my sister, I'm just not going to be able to sleep right until that someone is brought to justice."

"I don't know, Nadine. . . ."

"At least say you'll think about it. . . . I mean, all you have to do is spend a few days . . . just, like, looking into the possibility. I even hear that you're getting along with Toni and Melissa now. Maybe you can talk to them. They won't give me the time of day. . . . Never did, never will. I don't think two snootier girls exist anywhere in the universe."

"You're right about that."

"Then you'll do it."

Diane looked at Nadine. The younger girl wore her sincerity on her sleeve. What harm would it do to ask a few questions here and there? She was certain nothing untoward would turn up—but maybe it would make Nadine feel better about Lynn's death.

And maybe, just maybe, it would make Diane feel better.

"All right, Nadine. But just for a few days . . ."

"Oh, thank you! Thank you so much!"

"But you'll have to tell me everything you know. . . . All of Lynn's friends and enemies . . . everything that could give a clue to why someone would—"

"Of course, of course." She pulled out another notebook and showed her a list of names. "I've already started listing all of Lynn's friends and acquaintances and jobs and, well, we can talk out the rest."

Diane took the list. "Thanks. But could we do that later on?" She looked at the clock and winced. "Right now, I have to study!"

*   *   *

Murder.

Diane couldn't get the word out of her mind.

Murder.

She wanted to reject the idea. Murder just didn't happen in a high school . . . not a good middle-class high school in the American heartland like Maxville High. Suicide, yes—teen suicide was a disease that struck everywhere. But not murder. That was just unthinkable.

It was after seventh period, and Diane had taken her history test. She hadn't done well, but now that didn't seem all that important. There were bigger things on her mind.

Murder, for one thing.

Part of the reason she'd done poorly on the history test had been that her mind had kept casting back over the things that Nadine Rivers had been saying. And the question kept looming: If somebody killed Lynn, how had he or she done it?

But more to the point . . .

If somebody had killed Lynn . . .

Who had done it?

And, inevitably, she had to draw the conclusion that she was trying to deny: One of the victims of the Three Sisters' slander.

She tried to push this possibility out her head, since she didn't want to think of any of these people as a murderer. Certainly, however, a murder had to have a motive. . . .

And not only did these people have motive, she had heard a couple of them—Fiona and Heather— actually wish Lynn Rivers—specifically—*dead*.

Diane was thinking about this when it happened.

Although Maxville High was a sprawling suburban high school, one of its wings had three floors. Diane's seventh period history class was on the west side of the highest floor, and to get down to her first floor locker she had to walk down the hall and then down an echo filled stairwell.

Normally, the stairway would have had a few people on it even though it wasn't used as often as other stairways. However, Diane had stayed late to talk to Mr. Gert, her history teacher (to try to explain why she'd done so poorly on the test) and when she'd finally ventured out into the hall, the corridors were fairly deserted, and the stairwell was totally empty.

She'd noticed the wax stripper can earlier. The janitors had been doing some work on that end of the hall, and they'd been taking off some of the old wax and were probably going to do more work tonight. The can was a big thing. "Fifty Gallons" it read. Diane noticed it only peripherally as she passed it in a fog, thinking about possible murder.

Clang! CLUNK!

She noticed it big time when it came thunk-thunk-thunking down behind her as she was halfway down the first set of steps.

Startled, she turned, and saw the thing rolling and roaring down upon her, making the noise of a couple of bowling alleys.

She froze for exactly one moment, and then she ran, with a shriek.

Gravity just kept on pulling the can down after her, terrifying and enormous.

At the last moment possible, she grabbed hold of the post at the end of the steps and swung herself over the landing and partway down the next steps.

The can slammed into the wall, spun around, rolled back and forth and then was still.

Somehow, its seal, though battered, stayed in place. Somehow it didn't spill wax stripper all over her. Of course she'd rather be drenched in chemicals than *dead* but all the same . . .

She took a deep breath.

She'd never been quite so close to death. If that can had caught her right, slammed her into the wall, it would have *crushed* her, smashed her good.

Later, thinking about it, Diane realized that if she'd been any further up the steps, the wax can probably *would* have gotten her.

One thing there could be no doubt of, she thought, catching her breath there, looking at that big can. Lynn Rivers *didn't* commit suicide!

And whoever had killed her, had just tried to kill Diane as well!

4

Diane sipped thoughtfully on her chocolate shake.

"I don't know, Diane," said Adam. "I really don't think you should get involved."

Clatter of dishes in the background. Sweet dairy smells. "Heartbreak Hotel." Laughter.

They were sitting in a local school hangout, an old-fashioned railroad-type diner called the Fifties Shack, at the corner of Elm and Henley. The joke around school was that only squares hung out there, since they only played old stuff like Elvis Presley on the jukebox—but it was so comfortable and the food was so good that it was a real fun place to bring a date, even if it wasn't hip. So most of the students at Maxville found themselves patronizing the place, cool or uncool.

It was a double Dutch chocolate shake she sipped.

And it was good. *Real* good.

Fortunately for her figure she wasn't a real sweet fiend . . . but she did have a weakness for chocolate—an urge she had to satisfy at least once a day. The shakes at the diner were rich and chocolaty enough to serve as a snack all by themselves.

She wasn't thinking much now about the size of her waistline or threats to her hips.

"Adam—I'm not talking to you to get your opinion. I'm here to get your *help*."

It had been a whole day since the incident with the can of wax stripper, and she'd started the preliminary questioning of people. However, it hadn't taken long to figure out that: (A) this was a bigger job than she could handle alone; and (B) if there was really someone out to kill her—or at least stop her from snooping—then she was going to have to call in some muscle.

And who better to qualify than her football-playing boyfriend? Unfortunately, it was pretty clear that Adam wasn't going to be as accommodating as she'd hoped.

"Look, Nancy Drew, if this thing about that barrel is really true—"

"It *is* true!"

"Okay, then, you should just not get involved. Go to the police, tell them what you know . . . and then take a vacation or something. Get out of here for a while."

"But I told you . . . there's no evidence to show the police, Adam! That's why Nadine came to me! That's what I have to dig up!"

Adam looked at her doubtfully. "How do you know you can trust Nadine's judgment on this?"

She pushed her shake away and started getting up. "Look, if you're going to be this way, Adam, maybe we should just forget my request. In fact, maybe we'd just better forget this whole *relationship*."

Adam grabbed her and pulled her back down onto the vinyl seat. "Oh come on, Diane, don't get upset.

It's because I *care* about you so much that I don't want you to do it."

"Look, Adam. I don't care whether or not you care so much—" She glared at him. "I'm going to do this investigation! Are you going to help me or aren't you?"

Now it was Adam's turn to get upset. His face got kind of funny red and he frowned, his teeth grinding a bit.

Generally, Adam was a pretty affable guy, always ready with a grin and a wisecrack. But sometimes, when they argued, she saw that Adam could get angry like everyone else, and it startled her a bit.

"You're so obstinate!" Adam said. "I can't stand when you get like this! Don't you understand, this may be something that is too dangerous for you. I'm not going to let you get involved in this kind of stuff, Diane!"

"I really appreciate your concern," said Diane firmly. "And I'm sorry if I sound obstinate. But this is really important, Adam. Someone was *murdered!*"

"Okay. Tell me. Why is it so all-fired important, huh?" Adam shook his head. "Okay, I mean, it is important, sure, because if somebody killed somebody, he or she should be brought to justice. But what I'm talking about is why this is so important to *you,* why *you* want to get involved so much. I mean, Lynn Rivers was hardly your best buddy."

Diane shook her head and let her chin drop. "To be perfectly honest, I can't help but feel . . . responsible."

"What? Where the heck do you get that from?"

"I don't know . . ." said Diane. "Maybe it was this battle of barbs I was having with the Evil Sisters that was the start of it all—maybe not, sure. But I can't help feeling that maybe . . . well, you know, that if I hadn't done the things I did, said the things I said . . . that maybe Lynn would be alive today.''

"That's . . . that's nonsense,'' said Adam.

"You know, she really wasn't a bad person. She didn't deserve to die.''

"Nobody deserves to die. But we all do it. . . .''

"Hopefully after about eighty years of a good life. But Lynn died much too soon. She deserves to be remembered . . . well, not as someone who gave up. So I'm going to prove that she didn't give up, that someone was responsible for her death.''

"Stubbornness may make a good private detective, but it's pretty darned annoying in a girlfriend.''

She scooted off the seat and started storming away.

"Okay, Mr. Bravery. It's clear that you don't want to get involved because you're afraid yourself. As for me . . .'' She tossed her head and strutted away. "I'll have you know I can take care of myself!''

She stalked away from Adam, leaving him with a stunned look on his face. In the six months they'd been dating, she'd been free-spirited, sure—but she'd never shown her independence quite to this degree.

She didn't even give Adam time to say he was sorry before she was out the door, leaving him with his shock—and the bill to boot.

Eerie. Deserted, haunted. Yet bearing traces of perfume and bits and pieces of a life.

Lynn's room was almost exactly as Diane had seen it before.

"They left it kind of messed up," explained Nadine. "The police, I mean. They had to look around, you know. . . . But when they were finished, I tried to put things back, the way they had been. . . ." Nadine sat down on the frilled bed and sadly petted one of the several stuffed animals that sat there—a tiger. "This was Mr. Tail-bow. Lynn's favorite. When I was little she let me play with the others—but never Mr. Tail-bow."

"What did the policemen find?" said Diane, nervously draining her Coke and placing the can in the wastebasket.

"Nothing amiss, they said."

"What about fingerprints? Here . . . or in the bathroom?"

"Oh, they hardly made any kind of effort. The detective in charge, Lieutenant Glickert—he made what he called a 'cursory dusting' at the scene."

"The bathroom?"

"Yeah. Anyway, he didn't find any fingerprints. I mean, not even Lynn's."

Diane frowned. "That's weird."

"Yes, *tell* me about it. But when I asked him about that, he just shrugged it off—'Bathrooms often don't take prints,' he said. 'Besides, this one looks like it gets cleaned a lot.' Which is true, because Lynn was always very particular about that."

"Sounds kinda odd to me. . . ."

"Me too. And I said so. But they said, 'Hey, you're just a kid. We're the pros here.' "

"Oh, right." Diane sighed. "Well, it did look pretty much like a straight suicide. I should know. . . ."

"But you know now that it wasn't. . . ."

Diane had told Nadine about the wax stripper can incident.

"Yes," Diane said. "We both know for sure. But there's no proof."

"Not even that can coming after you?"

"Nope. They could say that was an accident—or even that I set it up myself."

"I don't understand. . . . Why didn't they do a more thorough investigation?"

"I guess Lynn's death was trouble enough. They didn't want to delve any deeper."

Nadine sniffed back a tear. "Well, I guess we're going to have to make them, aren't we?"

"Yes, I guess we will." She looked into the bathroom which no longer bore any trace of the grisly event that had occurred there. "It's obvious to me, though, that the bathroom was cleaned *after* the murder. I mean, I noticed it was *spotless*. Even if your sister was meticulous she wouldn't have cleaned it that much . . . not if she was planning to kill herself, right?"

"I agree totally," said Nadine, relief that Diane was taking her seriously showing in her voice. "Lynn was very up in her letters. She gave absolutely no indication that she was even considering something drastic like suicide. . . ."

"Wait a minute, though," said Diane. She looked around at the bathroom and shivered. No reason to be in here, there were no clues—and lots of reasons *not* to be in here, paramount of which was that it was so *creepy*. Every time she looked at that clean, sparkling bathtub, all she could see was Lynn Rivers in the bloody water.

"Yes?" said Nadine.

"First, let's get out of here. Mind if we go to your room?"

"That's a good idea." Clearly the room gave Nadine problems as well.

Nadine's room was typical of a teenager's sleeping quarters. There were pictures of various stars and groups cut from *Tiger Beat* and the place had the disheveled look of a mind confused in the mazelike corridors it had to travel toward adulthood. Piles of books and comics cluttered the desk, and a complicated network of tubing and plastic cages held a colony of pet gerbils. Their scent mingled with the scent of perfume and the smell of dirty socks.

Diane immediately felt much more comfortable.

Nadine cleared some schoolbooks off the chair in front of the desk and indicated that Diane should sit.

"Okay. We can talk freely in here. I've checked. My parents can't hear anything from where they are. What were you going to say to me, Diane?"

Diane sat down thoughtfully. "Okay. From all indications your sister, Lynn, did not act depressed. In fact, from her letter and her behavior she seemed up."

"That's right."

"But I saw Lynn a few times over the past couple months, and quite often she seemed—well, not exactly down, but most definitely preoccupied."

"You mean, like she was thinking about something else?"

"Yes. And she didn't seem at all happy about what she was thinking about either."

Nadine thought about this seriously for a moment and then nodded gravely. "You're right. Now that you mention it, sometimes Lynn did seem aloof and concerned about something. But depression is different from being concerned. There are lots of different signs. I know, I've been depressed before, haven't you?"

"Sure," said Diane, "but nothing serious. No, that's not what I'm talking about, though. What I mean was that Lynn might have been—what's the word for it—manic-depressive."

Nadine rejected that out of hand. "No. Lynn was lots of things, but she was certainly never manic."

"Okay. Then there must have been another reason for the moods we both noticed."

Nadine nodded grimly.

"She knew that she was in danger," said Diane. "She knew that someone wanted to kill her."

"But who?" said Nadine, a tear starting to drip from her eye. "Who'd want to do that?"

"That," said Diane, "is what I intend to find out."

5

Maxville had been a small town, until the encroaching suburbs of the neighboring megalopolis swept its highways past, making it a bedroom community for city workers. Still, it retained much of its small town charm and flavor, and several of its neighborhoods still looked pretty much as they'd looked forty or fifty years ago: large solid Victorian houses set like monuments to a bygone age amid oaks and poplars and parks.

The Ayers family lived in one such house. It was to this house that Diane drove the Saturday morning after her discussion with Nadine. She'd made an appointment to talk with the remaining Evil Sisters, and she hoped it would be productive.

It was a gloomy fall morning. The sun only occasionally peaked out from behind the clouds. The air smelled of burning leaves and the oncoming winter.

Not the most promising of days, certainly, but appropriate for the task before her—investigating the possible murder of Lynn Rivers.

As she hummed along in the sporty little Toyota that her parents often let her use now that she had her driver's license, she wondered if maybe Adam wasn't right. Should she just go to the police and tell them what happened? Or maybe just write it all up in her column and then wash her hands of it? Why was this becoming an obsession with her? Why was she doing a junior Lois Lane number here—and with no Superman to back her up!

By the time she'd pulled into the Ayers's driveway, though, she'd figured out the answer.

It wasn't just the reporter's desire to undercover the truth, and it wasn't just because she had a sense of justice to play out. No, it was because, deep down, she realized that she had *felt* something for Lynn Rivers. She knew that Lynn could well have been she—she understood how it was that a "nice" person could get wrapped up in sleazy gossip mongering, mixed up with snooty people like Toni and Melissa. She could sympathize because she'd almost done it herself.

And whatever she and the Sisters had done, Lynn Rivers did not deserve to die for it! Diane got out of her Toyota that morning more sure than ever that she was doing the right thing.

Toni Ayers herself answered the door.

"Well, I see it's a dress-down Saturday for everyone!" said the petite brunette casually eyeing Diane's old jeans, sweatshirt, and lack of makeup. Toni, on the other hand, was dressed in loose-fit designer jeans, a crisp white cotton blouse, black Reebok athletic shoes, and a silk scarf around her neck, all the height of fashion.

"Come into the parlor," she continued, leading Diane through the impeccably furnished living room, filled with expensive antiques all polished to high gloss, Diane was sure, by a cleaning service. "Melissa is waiting."

The "parlor" was less ostentatious, actually the family room, filled with a wide-screen television set, a state-of-the-art audio system, computers, and other techno toys.

"My dad's," Toni explained.

"MTV Raps" was on the TV, the cadenced rhythms chug-a-chugging from huge speakers.

"Melissa," shouted Toni, "would you turn that nonsense down please? Diane's here." She turned smartly to her guest. "You have to excuse Melissa. I'm trying to break her of this habit, but she seems peculiarly addicted to this odd specimen of pop culture. Print that in 'Dying to Know' if you want. I'm sure that will be a nice little nugget for your friends."

Melissa thumbed down the volume of the TV and turned around on the plush couch to face Diane. She wore nice jeans and a silk blouse and long, dangly earrings.

Diane wondered if the Evil Sisters even slept in jewelry and designer PJs.

"Hello, Diane," Melissa said coolly. She seemed distracted, and Diane realized that Toni's attitude was—well, like makeup. Covering up something. But what?

"Would you care for a Coke or something?" offered Toni, sitting down and staring with distaste at the sneakered and sweatshirted rappers bounced about silently, chains swinging willy-nilly.

"No thanks, I'm fine." Diane sat down on the edge of the couch, trying to find the right words to say.

"So we're here and you're here," said Melissa. "What do you want, Diane?"

"It's about Lynn."

Suddenly, their veneers cracked. They bowed their heads and Diane could see the beginnings of tears in their eyes. Melissa had to look away and Toni had to speak for both of them. "Yes. Lynn. What about Lynn, Diane?"

It just all spilled out in one gush.

"I have reason to think that her death wasn't a suicide. I think that somebody killed her."

Melissa's head swung around with the speed of something mechanical. "What?"

"This is nothing to joke about!" Toni chimed in.

"Do I look like I'm joking? I'm serious, guys!" Diane could not hide her annoyance with them.

"But that's the police verdict . . . I mean, the cut wrists, the bathtub . . . the whole thing!" said Toni, blinking.

Quickly, tersely, Diane explained the evidence. She told them about Nadine, about the wax stripper can—and about her general gut feeling. But most important, she told them about motivation.

"I think that Lynn—and you two—hurt a lot of people. And one of those people killed her and made it look like a suicide. I think that your lives could be in danger too."

Melissa just stared into the air, her eyes glazing. Toni, however, got up and paced, fingernails dug into her palms. "You see! I told you it was a possibility!"

"I don't believe it!" Melissa said. "Why would anyone want to kill someone like Lynn!"

"It's hard to believe—but you know, people can

be scum," said Toni, looking a little nervous. "Sure, maybe Lynn did some things she shouldn't have. And yes . . . well, maybe we said some things too. . . . But we never really meant anyone harm— I mean, you just do what you do, and we're interested in people and we like to talk about them and . . ."

Toni went on and on. Diane had never seen her so nervous before. She had to interrupt.

"Okay. You agree that it's a possibility."

"It's hard to believe . . . hard to accept. . . . Maybe it was just Lynn that they were after," said Toni, gaining a little more control.

"I still don't think anyone killed her," said Melissa firmly. "I think she committed suicide."

"Can you afford the possibility that she didn't?" said Diane. "Can you afford the chance that maybe someone *did* kill her—and that maybe they'll be after you next?"

"She's right, you know," said Toni. She sat back down and took a deep breath. "You know, this is one of those times when I wish I smoked."

"That would kill you more slowly than revenge," said Melissa. "But it would kill you."

"All right," said Diane. "Who knows, maybe I'm wrong. And I certainly do hope that I am wrong. But we can't take that chance, and that's why I need your help. Let's face it, Toni and Melissa. You and Lynn did some people dirty, and you made some serious enemies. You created a lot of ill will and now it's coming back to haunt you. What I need is some concrete details. Are you willing to help?"

Melissa and Toni nodded. "Okay," said Toni. "I guess we owe that to Lynn. I mean, if someone

82

really did kill her, then we've got to help find the murderer."

"If there *is* a murderer," said Melissa stubbornly.

Diane agreed. "Okay. The first question, then, is if there is a murderer . . . why Lynn? Why not one of you two? Pardon me, but as an expert on the antics of the Evil Sisters. . ."

Toni stared coldly at her. "Please . . . we really hate that name. . . ."

"Okay. Anyway, of you all, Lynn was by far the least assertive in spreading malicious gossip."

"Whatever."

"Then you agree."

"Well, not necessarily. Look, like I said, we never meant to harm anybody. . . ." said Toni. "Lynn did her share of . . . talking, though."

"So do you think that we can narrow it down? Was there anyone you know whose hatred for you all focused specifically on Lynn?"

Toni shook her head, looking as though she were under a lot of strain. "Nooo . . ." Toni said slowly. But then her mouth took a bend that usually signaled the arrival of some barb or slur against someone. "Unless you count—"

Melissa clearly recognized that face, that tone even better than Diane. "Toni!" she said in an unusually stern voice for the second banana of the team. "No more rumors, remember? We've stopped that!" She turned to face Diane squarely. "Like we've said before, Diane. No more gossip, nothing except hard cold facts—and those only when we're sure they're not going to hurt anyone."

"I think that's wise," said Diane. "A bit like closing the barn door after the cows are gone, but I appreciate the attempt. But you know, in this case, I won't be spreading anything, and we need every bit, every scrap of possible evidence, so you should say what you were going to say. It might be important.''

Toni frowned.

Suddenly she looked absolutely miserable.

"The more I think about it," she said finally, "the more I can see your point. People *did* hate us, didn't they?" She shivered as though a cold wind had just passed over her spine. "And our words . . . our careless fun . . . it caused people harm. . . . And I don't want my words to hurt anyone anymore. But if I can help you find Lynn's murderer . . .''

With that, Toni Ayers began haltingly to talk about the people Lynn's words in particular had hurt.

6

She found Rick Elkins at home on Saturday, raking leaves.

A chill wind had sprung up from the east, and Diane had put on a warm ski parka. Rick, however, wore only a flannel shirt and that with the sleeves rolled up yet!

After reviewing her notes from her conversation with Toni and Melissa, Diane realized that she had four very strong suspects.

Namely, the Evil Sisters' most recent and most devastated victims.

Rick Elkins, Fiona MacKensie, Jim Stevens, and Heather Perkins.

And from what Toni and Melissa had said, hadn't they had gripes with Lynn in particular?

It was an unnerving confrontation with Rick. After making small talk for a while, Diane realized that the guy was raking the leaves into small piles that would be blown away again, and he didn't seem to notice at all that his work was for nothing.

This guy *was* kind of out of it.

Finally, Diane braced herself for the necessary

question. She felt uneasy bothering a guy who had a history of mental and emotional problems, and had only recently had some kind of breakdown. God alone knew what the Sisters' gossip about him had done!

Nonetheless, she'd promised herself to do the best job she could. She let fly.

"Rick—did you hear what happened to Lynn Rivers?"

Rick stopped raking. He looked up, and there was a nasty sneer on his face. "Yeah. Saves the world some grief. Too bad her buddies didn't take a leap into the bloody tub as well."

Strands of Rick's hair spiked up like a mop of thorns. He looked like Alec Baldwin on a bad day on a movie set, portraying a psycho. Diane felt more uncomfortable proceeding with her questioning, but she felt she had to. They were out in the open and there were cars passing by. If Rick were the killer, there was nothing he could do to her.

Not now, anyway.

"Rick—where were you that Sunday afternoon?"

Rick stopped raking and looked hard at Diane, realization flooding slowly into his eyes. "Oh. I get it. You think that I might have had something— Oh yeah, real cute . . . not a very nice thought, Diane. And here all the while I thought you were one of the only friendly people at Maxville High."

Diane did a double take, then she gave Rick a look as sincere as she could muster. "Did I accuse you of anything? Look, Rick, let's face it. You had good reason to dislike the Three Sisters—I can't blame you for that." She aimed the next statement directly at him. "And I've reason to believe that Lynn Rivers did *not* kill herself!"

Rick took that in total stride. "You think that someone did the world a favor, huh?" He shrugged. "Well, it wasn't me, Diane, if that's what you're thinking. I spent, like, the whole afternoon and evening at the college library. I can't be Mr. Popularity anymore—I might as well hit the books, huh?"

Defiance glimmered in his dark eyes.

"Thanks, Rick. I'm sorry to bother you. But I'm just trying to get to the bottom of this."

Rick looked at her in a funny way. "You know, if Lynn Rivers got off, maybe you'd better watch out who you go around questioning, hmmm?" Diane saw absolutely no concern in his expression. Only a cold lack of sympathy. "And the other two . . . maybe they've got something to worry about too, huh?"

"You're sounding awfully threatening! Do you mean to sound that way?"

"Threatening? Gee, I don't mean to sound that way. I'm just acting like I always do, Diane." He smiled. "Remember, I'm a disturbed soul, right?"

"Sometimes I think that's just an act, Rick."

"Act? You think I'm an actor? Well, I guess that's not such a bad thing, Diane. Heck of a lot better than a murderer!"

"I never said you were a murderer!"

"Maybe you'd better just not say anything for a while until you've got something a little more solid to base your suspicions on, hmmm!" He didn't look threatening at all now—just intense.

Diane shivered. She thanked Rick and got the heck

out of there. This guy definitely gave her the heebie-jeebies.

Her next stop was at the Maxville Junior College library.

This was a favorite place with local high school students for last minute cramming, since it was open on Sunday evening, whereas the public and high school libraries were closed. It was a large blocklike building with narrow slits for windows, very modern looking, surrounded by a lot of well-kept shrubbery, grass, and flower beds. Maxville Junior College was the newest establishment in the area and the current jewel. It even *smelled* new, just taken out of its plastic, Diane thought as she walked past the security pillars. Not very busy either today—she could see only a scatter of students at the desks, or at the shelves.

She went straight to the checkout counter, where a young woman in round-framed glasses, with stringy, curly brown hair, sat on a stool, hunched over a glossy copy of *Cosmopolitan.*

"Pardon me. Hi," Diane said, smiling. "I'm sorry to bother you."

"No problem." The girl was actually younger than she seemed at first. Probably she was a student here, only a few years older than Diane herself.

"Do you work here on Sunday nights?"

"Yeah. For my sins." The girl smiled. "I get Saturday and Friday nights off, so I guess that's what's important."

"Were you here last Sunday night?"

"Yeah, sure. Why?"

"I'm doing some detective work."

"Kind of young for that, aren't you?" The girl

didn't look as if she really wanted to get involved in anything serious, and Diane really couldn't blame her. She changed her tack to something more harmless and a lot more intriguing.

"Oh, this isn't Dick Tracy time. I'm just checking up on my boyfriend!"

"Oh!" The girl nodded in understanding and sympathy.

"He says he was here last Sunday night, but me, I think he was out with some other girl."

"Well he wasn't out with me—I was here!"

Diane laughed. She quickly described Rick Elkins to the girl, utilizing the powers of description she'd gained from journalism.

"Wow. I'd have remembered if I saw *that* guy," the library clerk said. "But nope . . . he wasn't here any of last Sunday, and I worked a ten-hour shift! Sounds like you have boyfriend problems!"

Diane sighed. "Believe me, I've got a lot more problems now than just that!"

Fiona MacKensie's house was a nice Cape Cod, tucked away from the neighbors by lots of shady oak trees. The day had started out sunny, but a number of clouds had gathered like omens. Diane had called ahead and been assured by Mrs. MacKensie that her daughter was home. The quiet, somber woman showed Diane through a subdued living room and hallway clustered with framed paintings and certificates of merit earned by various MacKensies. There was the smell of dried flowers and old perfume here, of stiff tradition. "We built Fiona her own study downstairs," said her mother softly. "Go on down. She's expecting you."

A study in the basement? It sounded rather depressing, thought Diane, who associated cellars with dampness, darkness, and cobwebs. However, the MacKensie basement was not totally underground—windows brought in what little light was available now on this gray fall day.

Fiona was sitting in a chair, just staring into the air. A book and papers were stretched over a desk. The Macintosh computer that Fiona used wasn't even turned on.

"Fiona—I thought you were working on your essays," said Mrs. MacKensie, her pleasantness extremely forced.

Fiona just tapped her temple. "In here, Mom. In here."

"Oh. Well, I'll leave you two alone then."

Fiona waited until her mother had left and then sighed and said, "Mothers!"

"I know what you mean! Mine tries so hard not to meddle but she can't help herself."

The study was tastefully decorated with prints from the city museum. There was a record player, and a number of classical records and cassettes were strewn about. Fiona got up and put on a Mozart tape. Diane, whose taste in music was fairly wide, thought it was a little strange for a sixteen year old to listen to only classical music—but, hey, she'd rather listen to Mozart than to rap, which she didn't like very much.

"You want a Coke?" said Fiona.

"Only if it's a Diet."

"Certainly. Absolutely no problem. There's an auxiliary refrigerator down here." She went and got them both Diet Cokes.

"So, Diane, what can I help you with?" said

90

Fiona, a little formally, sitting on the edge of her desk, taking up a pen and toying with it.

Diane took a swallow of her drink. "I'll make it short and to the point, Fiona. I've discovered evidence that suggests that Lynn Rivers did not commit suicide. In fact, I think she might have been killed."

"What?" Fiona said, looking up from her drink, clearly startled at the very notion. "Oh my God—what a dreadful thought. Murder . . . Who would—" She cut herself off short, immediately seeing the implication. "You don't think that if that's the case, that *I* could possibly have anything to do with it, do you?"

"I don't know, Fiona. You sounded in an absolutely murderous mood that day at lunch hour, waiting for your ride!"

"Well, of course, what do you think . . . I mean . . . I was really quite angry, and you would have been too, in my place."

"Go on. I'm not accusing you of anything, I'm just letting you know about what I think is the situation here. Namely, that Lynn Rivers did *not* kill herself."

Fiona closed the book on the desk and absently chewed the eraser on her pencil for a moment. She shook her head. "Murder . . . No, it certainly *couldn't* have been me. You can ask the therapist I'm seeing . . . I'll give you her name if you like. I needed *someone* to get me through that whole business with Mr. Hughes. When I heard about Lynn . . . well, I cried because I realized that, well, that could have been *me*. . . . I've thought about ending it all before. . . . Thank heavens I never did but I thought . . . I sure understand how poor Lynn felt. . . . But now you say it could have been murder. That's very hard to accept. Very hard.''

"I know," said Diane ruefully. She didn't feel very good about this aspect of the situation at all. "So hard that the police don't accept it. Which means that I'm the one who has to dig up the facts. I'm the one who has to investigate the possibility."

"That's understandable," said Fiona. "So I suppose you're going to want my alibi, huh? Well, all I can say is thank the powers that be that I wasn't with Mr. Hughes in compromising circumstances." Fiona said this with a sarcasm that was unlike her. "I was right here, doing what I'm doing now. Studying. But I'd appreciate it if you wouldn't tell my witnesses to this fact—my mother and my father, my brothers and sisters—that you suspect me. If I really need them, like with the police, I'll call upon them. But really, now that they think I might be a tart, I don't want them considering me a murderer as well."

Diane could sympathize with this wish, and she let it go at that, leaving the girl to her studies—or to her woolgathering.

However, something definitely troubled her about Fiona. It made her slightly suspicious. In all likelihood, she was telling the truth—but if not, it would make sense that a girl who had thought a lot about suicide would know how to stage a murder to look like one.

Diane had never been really keen on bowling, or bowling alleys for that matter. It wasn't that she had anything against the noisy, beery atmosphere of the places. It was just that she was never very good at throwing a black ball down a wooden alley to strike pins set up in a triangle.

So when she entered the clattering, bustling Maxville Bowlarama that Saturday afternoon, she was surprised by the boisterous life of it all. The smell of floor wax, shoe spray, spilled beer and Coke, and stale potato chips and french fries hung heavy in the air, along with cigarette smoke drifting from the lounge. The place was full and alive, and the sound of rolling balls and bursting pin formations surrounded her as she asked the attendant where she could find Jim Stevens's team. The guy, a cigar stub working in his thick lips, gave surly but accurate directions.

Jim Stevens was resting at a table just behind alley number ten.

"Jim," said Diane, "can I talk to you a moment?"

"Yo! Diane! What are you doing here?"

"To see you. Your dad said I could find you here!"

"Yep. Here and in a great mood, too. The Duckpin Maulers—that's my team, aren't they beautiful?" The remnants of the Maulers hailed Diane in good spirits. "The Duckies have just won two out of three against the incredibly feared Alley Cats."

The Duckies booed the name, and a few Cats called back, making rematch noises.

Jim chuckled. "You could say that I helped these jokers 'steal' it away. Got ten strikes out of thirty frames. Not bad for Duckpins, huh? Seems my klepto past is standing me in good stead!"

"We're checking for our wallets, buddy!" said an Alley Cat with good humor.

"You better!" Jim laughed.

"You seem unusually comfortable with your past, Jim," said Diane, impressed.

"Oh, yeah," Jim said, smiling after chugging back a large icy quantity of syrupy Coke from a paper cup. "It's all turned out real well."

The Rip van Winkle thunder of rolling balls and crashing pins and the smell of floor wax and shoe disinfectant began to recede into the background for Diane. Jim started to unlace his shoes as they talked.

"So you don't mind that the Evil Sisters spilled your secret," said Diane.

"Well, I know they didn't do it out of the kindness of their hearts," Jim said, stretching his muscular frame, flashing nice white teeth and blue eyes beneath his blond hair. "And at first I was really really upset and embarrassed. I mean, as you know, Diane, I'd worked real hard to put all that shoplifting stuff behind me. I don't know, maybe *too* hard. . . . It was making me all uptight and bothered, you know. I kept on having these nightmares that the truth would leak out and my whole life would crumble in shambles. Well, thanks to the work of the Sisters, it *did* get out—and my life *didn't* go down in complete shambles. Oh, there were a few rough spots, and I lost my job and all. But I've got a new job at the drugstore because Mr. Harris trusts me, he knows me—and well, now I don't have to agonize over the whole thing. It's all out in the open."

"People don't look at you like you're a thief?" asked Diane.

"Oh no. In fact, I've had lots of people, girls and guys alike, come up to me and tell me that *they've* shoplifted and felt bad about it and needed to confess

94

it to someone. Heck, one guy even asked for shop-lifting tips!"

"What did you say?"

"Stop it!" Jim grinned and finished his Coke.

"Terrible about Lynn Rivers, wasn't it?"

Jim nodded and frowned. "Yeah. You bet. You know, that was just awful. The thing is, nobody should die young, I mean *nobody*, I don't care how rotten they are. And she was the best of that bunch. And the thing is, well, Melissa and Lynn and Toni are just characters, every school has them. . . . They're not really bad, they just have a problem like I did."

"You seem very philosophic about the whole thing," said Diane. *Maybe almost* too *forgiving*, she thought. On one hand her basic good nature was happy for him—but on the other, this whole jolly attitude was, well, kind of suspicious and Diane didn't really feel good about it. "The thing is, Jim, I've got reason to believe that Lynn's death wasn't a suicide. It *might* have been murder."

Jim had been crunching his shaved ice. He stopped, his eyes filled with surprise. "What?"

"I'm not going to tell you why; the evidence isn't specific enough. I'm just letting you know so that maybe you can help me. The police don't seem to care, but I do—so I'm looking into the matter."

Jim swallowed the remainder of his ice and blinked. "Wait a minute. Just because they did something bad to me . . . I . . . I mean, you don't think—"

"I'm talking to everyone who was involved with Lynn in any way, Jim. I'm sorry."

Jim shook his head. "Bizarre. Look, I may have

been a petty thief, but I'm no . . . killer." He seemed to have difficulty getting the word out.

"I'm not accusing you of anything, Jim. I'm just—"

"Look . . . gee, what, you want an alibi?" He looked, suddenly a little ashen. "For what day, again? When did this happen?"

"Last Sunday."

Jim shook his head. "Well, I was . . . I was taking a drive. Out to the mountains, you know? I had to clear my head about some stuff."

"Did anyone go with you?"

"No. I needed to be alone. Hey—" He laughed. "What is this, 'Dragnet'? You sure don't look like the type. Sure. Diane 'Just the Facts' Delany!"

Diane didn't laugh. This stuff was far too serious to laugh about. "Thanks for your help, Jim."

"Any more questions, I'll be happy to answer them the best I can."

"You've been very helpful. I do appreciate it."

However, as she left, she thought to herself, *was* Jim Stevens being helpful? Or was it just a cover to hide guilt?

Who had done it?
Who killed Lynn Rivers?

Sunday had gotten cloudier. Dark and forboding. Diane spent it brooding and thinking.

Monday, it rained.

Not a thunderstorm. It was too far into fall for that. But in a way, Diane would have preferred thunder and lightning to the kind of steady, droning rain that came down resentfully, promising a steady daylong presence.

Now she sat in the auditorium, her boots pooling water below her, her raincoat dripping nearby, thinking about her inquiries of the weekend.

All the people she talked to had motives for killing Lynn, and none had a very good alibi. She had not been able to get hold of Heather Perkins. She'd been out of town for the weekend. But Diane knew exactly where she'd be on Monday morning. Like Heather, Diane arrived at school on an early bus. Before homeroom, the auditorium opened up for early arrivals. There people usually sat catching up on homework.

Diane didn't see Heather yet, but she was sure she'd show up.

Most troubling now was what she'd found out about Jim Stevens. Yesterday, after her dutiful Sunday afternoon chicken dinner with her parents, she'd driven past the Rivers's house, and found a neighborhood kid named Fred outside, building a birdhouse.

She'd introduced herself and come right out and explained that she was the one who had discovered Lynn Rivers's body.

"Yuck!" said Fred. "That must have been pretty gross!"

"Yes, as a matter of fact, it was. Tell me, Fred. Did you see anyone strange at the house last Sunday?"

"Nope. I was in the front yard most of the afternoon, raking leaves, so I could tell you."

"Oh. Okay. Thanks very much. Just checking."

"You think somebody offed Lynn?" Fred had suggested eagerly.

"No," Diane lied. "But there must have been a reason she killed herself. I liked Lynn, and I'd like to know."

"Come to think of it, you know, I did notice something kind of strange that day," Fred admitted.

"Oh?"

"Yeah. This guy . . . he kept on driving along the road. Back and forth. A few times."

"A guy? What did he look like?"

"Dunno. He looked kinda average, I guess. What a minute, he had light hair and he was in a Japanese car. That's all I remember."

She tried to get a better description from him, but couldn't. "Thanks anyway, Fred. I appreciate your help," she said, and ever since, she'd wondered, Could it have been Jim Stevens? It hadn't sounded like Rick Elkins, that was for sure. But it did sound like Jim Stevens.

Right now, she wanted to talk to Heather Perkins.

Diane wondered if she'd missed her, so she took her coat and her books and went to the other side of the auditorium.

Sure enough, there was Heather, in all her glory, getting a guy to help her with her algebra homework.

Blooming femininity definitely had its pluses. Even if the Sisters had made people think that Heather was a tramp, that didn't stop her allure from working on guys.

"Excuse me, Heather," Diane said, "but I really need to talk to you."

"Oh yeah, I got your messages on the phone machine."

"You got a minute?"

"Well, I do have to finish these problems!"

"I'll finish them for you, Heather!" said Bill Timmons eagerly. "I can imitate your handwriting, no problem."

"I really don't approve of other people doing my homework," she said, clearly for Diane's benefit. She gave him her math book. "But just this once."

Bill scooted off, leaving them alone. Diane presented Heather immediately with the situation. There were only a few minutes until homeroom.

"Lynn . . . *killed?*" Heather shook her head in disbelief. "That's a pretty hard concept to swallow. I mean, it's hard enough to accept that she's dead . . . but *murdered*. That only happens in mystery stories. . . ."

"I only wish that were true."

Heather did a belated double take. "Oh gosh—I see now. After all those things—I guess you think I must be a suspect. You think I might have killed Lynn!"

"I'm just asking people questions, Heather. The police certainly aren't."

"I can understand that. Okay, I can answer questions, I guess. I bet the first one is, where were you that awful Sunday? Well let me see—Sunday mornings I go to church. I eat Sunday dinner with my parents—chicken usually."

"I had chicken with mine just yesterday," said Diane.

"Why is it always chicken? Anyway, then I take a nap and I do my homework, so that I can read Sunday night and watch 'Masterpiece Theater' and whatever other British shows are on PBS afterwards like 'Emma Thompson' or 'Alexei Sayle's Stuff.' " Heather was an Anglophile. "And then I read."

"Just Sunday afternoon."

"That would be sleeping and studying then. Gosh, Diane, I *guess* my parents could testify to that. . . .

But I don't know if they exactly *saw* me doing that. I mean, I suppose I could have slipped out the window and killed Lynn. But this isn't that kind of questioning, right? You're not the police."

"Sounds like something that would be difficult to do, since you're on the second floor, right?"

"That's right."

Heather Perkins announced all this with a kind of honesty and openness that squashed most of Diane's suspicions.

At the sound of the bell, Heather leaped to her feet.

"Oh dear! I'm supposed to meet Sheila in the art room. 'Bye. Talk to you later."

And before Diane could say or do much of anything more, Heather Perkins had scooted past her and out the door.

"Heather!" said Bill Timmons, behind her by a few seconds, caught up in the crush of students sweeping out the exit toward homeroom and the true beginning of the school day. He tripped, and the book dropped from his hands. Papers folded neatly and tucked between the leaves spilled out.

Diane hurried over and helped Bill pick them up. She couldn't help noticing that one of the papers was a cut-out section of the *Trumpet*. She unfolded it, discovering a black-and-white picture of Lynn Rivers. It was from earlier in the year when Lynn had been involved with a canned food drive which the media had covered. Diane remembered that Toni and Melissa had given Lynn a hard time about being a goody two-shoes for weeks afterwards.

In the photograph, Lynn's eyes were exed out. Magic Marker knives were stuck into her head and torso, as though to change the photo into something you might find in *Fangoria* magazine.

At the bottom, in Heather's angry scrawl, was written in the same black Magic Marker: ''Lynn, you DIE!!!''

7

The day had turned gray and forlorn, a bleak reminder that winter was seeping through the cracks. Days would be short. Night would clamp down like prison bars by five o'clock in the afternoon.

Diane paused on the public library steps. A sudden surge of cold swept through her. She shivered and wrapped her coat around her closer, although it did absolutely nothing to help. She felt momentarily paralyzed, as though all the stress of this private investigation had suddenly dropped on her head.

"You okay, miss?" said a concerned older man in a bow tie, stopping on the stone steps when he saw Diane leaning over the metal bar, grimacing.

"Yes. Thank you. Just a cramp. I'll be okay."

The man nodded and proceeded down to the parking lot, carrying his checked-out books in a worn cloth bag.

Diane straightened, took a deep breath, and then took each step slowly. *A walk,* she thought to herself. *I need a walk.* At the bottom of the steps, instead of heading out to the parking lot, she took a sharp right past a stand of oak trees and bushes and walked out to the city common. Kids and squirrels played here, mothers walked their babies in strollers, and old men fed pigeons. The common was an open area, so it held the light longer. Somehow, though, it didn't do much good. Diane felt all dark inside.

Stress.

Diane could feel the stress wringing her out like an old threadbare rag. She felt the fabric of herself tearing a bit at the seams.

This "investigation" wasn't turning out the way it was supposed to. Dragging on, becoming frustrating, it was tying her emotions up in knots. She wished she had never started it—but she knew, in her heart of hearts, she had no choice.

At the other side of the common were a few old, palatial houses, and in the front yard of one a man in a plaid jacket was burning leaves. Maxville had just passed an ordinance against burning leaves. In another two weeks, you would have to put your leaves out at the curb for collection. The man stood over the fire, watching it intently as though savoring one of his very last leaf fires. His eyes glowed red, reflecting the flames, and he held his rake like Satan with a pitchfork.

Diane stood at a nearby tree, leaning against it, watching one of the final rites of this time-honored tradition. She stood well back. She feared fire. It had been in just such a leaf fire that she'd burned her hand as a child, and ever since then she'd had a morbid fear of flames. Something kept her staring at the fire now, though. There was something arresting and dazzling about it.

Things were getting weird, no doubt about that. So much so that she found that she couldn't write her column anymore. So today she'd asked if she could take some time off. The editor, Joe Taglia, had agreed reluctantly, since "Dying to Know" was the most popular part of the *Trumpet*. Instead he'd assigned her to do a piece on the Harrelson family, who'd founded Maxville. The ninetieth anniversary of the town was coming up, and Joe was doing a special issue. This was why Diane was at the Central Public Library—she was researching the article in old town records.

She hadn't done much though. She was overwhelmed by a sense of doom and despair.

"The flames—they're very beautiful, aren't they?" said the man in the plaid jacket, turning to Diane. He spoke with beautiful diction, like an actor, but the result just gave Diane the creeps.

"Uhm—ah—yes."

"Would you like to stand—closer?" said the man.

"No. Thank you."

"Are you sure? It's getting chilly. I won't bite." The man smiled at her, and suddenly he looked incredibly sinister.

"I really have to go. Thanks anyway." She almost ran away from the man, who looked after her shaking his head.

"I'm sorry," he called after her. "I didn't mean to alarm you. . . ."

She kept her back to him and said nothing, even though she was thinking, *Why am I* acting *this way?* She knew why. She was acting this way because she was getting totally *paranoid*, that was why. She had to get *hold* of herself and straighten out if she was going to have *any* hope of finding out who had killed Lynn Rivers.

Still, the dusky afternoon had that creepy before-the-storm feel to it. She'd just have to ignore it. As she walked to her car, she occupied herself with thinking about the defaced picture that had fallen out of Heather's book. That kind of visual statement of anger from a sixteen year old wasn't all that unusual, come to think of it. It didn't mean that Heather actually had wanted to kill Lynn—not necessarily. Goodness knew, Diane herself had messed with many a picture of rivals, as well as drawn shooting stars, halos, and other grafitti around magazine and newspaper pictures. This, after all, was a form of modern American doodling, right?

Still, in conjunction with the fact that Lynn Rivers in all probability had been murdered, Heather's doodle didn't put her in a particularly good light.

Diane's keys jingled as she got them out of her purse. She had a lot of keys, most of which were useless, all strung on a purple key chain with a small penlight whose battery was dead. She opened the door of the Toyota and got in. She was feeling better already, and popping the channel to WROK helped. A Tom Petty song was jangling away, and that improved her mood immensely. She'd parked under a bunch of maple trees; dying leaves had fallen on the windshield and she swept them aside with her windshield wipers. She'd parked in a corner of the parking lot, out of view of the ivy-covered brick library because the lot had been full, but now it had emptied quite a bit. Unable to shake off completely her uneasy feeling, she locked her side door.

The Maxville Central Public Library was perched at the highest point of the town, adjacent to Main Street. This part of Main Street had been dubbed

"Rice-a-Roni Mountain" by the locals, since it was comparable to some of the streets of San Francisco. Sometimes when it really snowed hard, the police would rope it off from traffic and let kids sled down its steep slope.

Diane put her brake on to wait for a car to go past. The brake squeaked and made a funny sound. Dad had warned her that the car probably needed new brake pads. Of course, when you were not only trying to keep your grades up but also working on a paper *and* heading a one-person murder investigation, you didn't have much time for automobile maintenance.

Still, it didn't sound real good. Perhaps she should make the time. Or maybe she should just get Dad to do it.

Midway down the hill Diane applied the brakes at a stoplight. She heard a *snap!* from below the Toyota. Her foot and the brake pedal went straight to the floor. Diane's foot slipped to the gas pedal.

The car lurched ahead.

Diane, horrified, took her foot off the gas and instinctively tried the brake again, to no avail. After a moment of shock, she pulled the emergency brake up. But that had always been bad, and going down a hill at thirty plus miles an hour now, it didn't work at all. Before she had a chance even to downshift to slow herself a bit, she barreled straight through the stop sign, right into traffic. A truck reared up before her, an almost certain crash. Fighting off panic, she spun the wheel, swerving past the thing.

Gaining speed, she seemed to be flying down the hill now. If there had been any ice on the road, that would have been the end of her. *Keep your head!*

she thought. *Keep your head*. She kept the wheel straight and she downshifted by stages into first, slowing somewhat. But each downshift threatened to skid the car out of balance. The car weaved and lurched, bucking awfully, its wheels screeching as she tried to use a swerving tactic to slow it down.

An eternity later, drenched in sweat, she was at the bottom, going sixty miles an hour.

She swept through the red stoplight at Adams Street. It took all of Diane's willpower to keep her eyes open. Desperately, she looked around. The only car in sight was a red Ford sedan, but it was coming straight at her! She honked her horn desperately to warn the driver (why hadn't she done that on the way down? Oh yeah—she'd been too busy driving!) and she yanked the wheel around.

The wheels turned so hard that the car did a complete screeching three-hundred-and-sixty-degree turn. The car came out of it still going, but considerably slower. Fortunately, she was near an empty stretch of curb.

The wheel rammed the curb. The Toyota went up onto the sidewalk and the back wheels hit, bouncing Diane up so that she hit the top of her head on the ceiling. But not hard—and the seat belt held her so she didn't go out the window when the car jerked to a complete stop, the tailpipe and muffler screeching along the cement.

She sat for a moment in shock. Then she took in one, two, three deep breaths and tried to collect herself. Her nerves were shattered, but nonetheless, she felt finally able to get out of the car. Her legs were wobbly, but she was just happy that she was still in one piece.

She looked around. No flashing cop bubble tops. No stopped passersby, no halted cars—not even the Ford she'd almost hit.

Lingering in her mind was that terrible snapping sound.

She got down on her knees and looked under the car.

They lay along the side of the wheels like metal ropes: brake cables, snapped. No, not snapped—if they had snapped the ends would have been rougher. That icy feeling returned to the back of her spine, only colder.

No. These cables hadn't snapped. They'd been *cut*.

Diane paced nervously in the police precinct waiting room. She took a sip from her Orange Slice can, then put it down on the table. "Dad, you know, this really isn't necessary."

"Isn't necessary!" said April Delany, looking up adamantly from her seat in a worn metal chair. "Somebody tries to *kill* you, and reporting it to the authorities isn't *necessary?*"

Diane gave her father a why-did-you-have-to-tell-Mom look.

"I saw those brake cables, Diane. You can't deny that someone was trying to do you harm," said Mr. Delany. "I can't believe that you pursued this ridiculous investigation of yours. Clearly, though, things are out of control. You've *got* to tell the police what you told me about your suspicions."

"And don't forget about that awful can being pushed down the stairwell too!" said Mrs. Delany, jangling her keys like worry beads.

Now that she was calmer, Diane wished she hadn't told her father the whole truth. But for a while, after she'd called him and gotten the AAA to tow the car to a garage, she'd needed someone to support her. Instead of holding her and telling her it was okay, though, her father had hit the roof. He'd sternly told her that she'd made a very bad mistake by even thinking about carrying out any kind of investigation and that she should go to the police about it immediately and turn the matter directly over to them. Then he'd told her mother, and Diane had to tell the whole story again, to a far more hysterical ear.

All in all, not a good day.

Now here she was on Tuesday morning, missing her morning classes so that she and her parents could make a formal complaint. Finally, she could transfer the burden of this investigation into hands more capable than hers.

"I won't forget any of it." Diane sighed. "I'll tell them everything." She meant that, too—she wanted *out* of this whole thing. She'd done her job— the fact that someone wanted to kill her *proved* that someone had killed Lynn Rivers, right?

The police would have to accept that for a fact now.

Five minutes later, a balding man in a wrinkled white shirt and a shoulder holster opened the door. In an ink-stained hand he held a piece of paper which he read through half-frame glasses. "Diane Delany?"

"That's her!" said April Delany. "Someone's trying to kill her. You've got to do something."

Mr. Delany puffed his chest out importantly. "I'm Diane's father and a member of the—"

The man scowled at Mr. Delany and cut him off. "Diane, you sixteen?"

"Yes, sir."

"Good. We don't need your parents in here. Their signed complaint's enough." The man pushed the door open and beckoned her. "You folks study the five-year-old copies of *Reader's Digest* out here. There *will* be a quiz."

"But—" said Mr. Delany.

"Really!" said Mrs. Delany.

The man slammed the door on them. He walked back to his desk and sat in his chair, picking up a large mug of coffee and sipping it as he studied the formal complaint. He offered Diane no coffee. Finally, he looked up at her. "You like to stand?"

"No." There was a chair in front of the desk. Diane sat down, wishing she had brought her keys to worry.

The office was small and colorless. There was a picture of a pained looking woman holding two frowning babies on the desk by a huge stack of folders and a stack of reports. The place smelled of burnt coffee and old donuts. A coat and a hat hung on a rack in the corner.

"I'm Lieutenant Detective Hawkins, Diane. The original detective assigned the Rivers suicide is off this week."

"But it wasn't a suicide. . . . It—"

"I'm a busy guy, Diane. But I'm on my coffee break. Says here you think that someone's trying to kill you. How come?"

Diane sighed. Carefully and as concisely as possible, she told the police detective the whole story. It was difficult because Hawkins stared at her with slightly bulging eyes the whole time, hardly blinking.

When she was finished, he sipped his coffee and then put the mug down on the table. "Wax stripper can down the stairwell. Cut cables. A line of suspects and rampant paranoia . . ." He grunted and dug something out of his ear. "I think, Diane Delany, that you've been reading entirely too many Agatha Christie novels."

Agatha Christie novels!

"You don't believe Lynn Rivers didn't commit suicide?"

The lieutenant detective shook his head. "It's not a matter of belief, Ms. Delany. It's a matter of facts. There are absolutely no facts involved with Lynn Rivers's death that have lead anyone but you to the conclusion we have a murder here."

"But Nadine . . . Nadine Rivers. The letter . . . !"

"Ms. Delany, you've never dealt with suicide in a family before, and I hope you never have to again. Family members are loathe to admit the possibility that a loved one offed herself! Apparently this is the case with Nadine Rivers. Why, pray tell, didn't she show the police this letter—"

"She did! But they told her it wasn't sufficient evidence."

Hawkins grunted. "Wouldn't know about that—wasn't on the case. But it sounds pretty flimsy to me!"

"But why would someone be trying to kill me?" said Diane, exasperated.

"Well now, these incidents you report are a rather grave matter. And we'll put them on report. We'll keep in touch with you and send an officer over later to speak to the authorities at school. However, there's nothing that you told me to conclude that this has anything to do with the fictitious murder of Lynn Rivers, unless one of the kids you questioned got insulted by your accusations." He leaned over, his eyes slits of suspicion. "Or what's to say that you didn't cook this up yourself to get us back into this so-called investigation."

"Pardon me, sir, but I think that now *you're* the one who's being paranoid."

"Maybe." The lieutenant sniffed. He pulled out a pack of Juicy Fruit gum and unwrapped two sticks. He popped both into his mouth. "You say you're the gossip columnist for your high school paper. Maybe you just ticked some people off, and they're getting even."

"By trying to kill me?"

"You look alive to me. I admit, these things sound serious and like I say we'll keep an eye out for you, Ms. Delany." He chomped his gum loudly. "But I don't think we're going to call out the FBI on this one just yet. Thanks for dropping by."

Diane shook her head in disbelief. "That's it! Somebody tries to kill me and you still don't believe that Lynn Rivers was murdered!"

"In a word, nope! Good day, Ms. Delany!" He took the papers he'd been referring to and stuffed them into the Out box. "Oh and by the way, just on a personal note—maybe if there is someone steamed at you for this gossip stuff, you should just lay off for a while, hmm?"

"I have, Lieutenant," she said. "I have."

She'd show them, she thought as she left. And

most especially, she'd make this jerk Lieutenant Detective Hawkins *eat* that stupid report!

She went out to face her parents.

Adam Grant was pretty upset.

"Look, Diane, what did I tell you? You stick your nose where it doesn't belong, you might get it cut off!"

"Spare me the original thinking," said Diane nervously as she paced Adam's family room. She'd come over to confide her problems to him, to maybe get some help—and what was she getting in return? A lecture ridden with clichés!

"Diane, you admit—you're in trouble. And you're in trouble because somebody doesn't want you to be snooping around about this Lynn Rivers business!"

Diane stamped her foot defiantly. "Because the person who *killed* Lynn doesn't want to be found out!"

"Is that what the police said?"

"No."

"Look, Diane, they're the professionals. They're the experts. Why don't you believe them? You know, I realize that you haven't thought about this, but there's a very strong possibility that whoever's behind these attempts to frighten you—"

"Attempts to *frighten* me? They're attempts to *kill* me!"

"Well, they haven't killed you, and they seem pretty lame to me. I mean, if someone wanted to kill you, there are a lot more effective ways than cutting your brake cables!"

"You didn't see the size of that truck that almost creamed me! A lot you care, Adam Grant!" She was

113

on the verge of tears. "And I thought you were my boyfriend. Boyfriends are supposed to care if you almost get killed."

Adam sighed. He went over and he put his arms around her. Diane at first was stiff and reluctant, but Adam's strong hold and his smell held their old appeal for her, and she found herself melting against him.

For a few long moments of silence it was the old Diane and Adam magic. She wished that she could just wrap herself up in it and forget the world forever.

However, the moment could not last.

"Diane, of course I care about you," said Adam softly. "But please—for everyone's sake, you've got to stop this weird obsessive investigation of yours."

Diane stiffened. "I can't."

"You can't! What, don't you have free will? What, are you some kind of robot or something?"

Diane pushed him away. "No, Adam. I can't because I've promised people. I've promised Nadine, I've promised the spirit of Lynn Rivers—and most importantly, I've promised *myself* that I'm going to get to the bottom of this!"

"You are the stubbornest, most foolhardy person I've ever met!" said Adam, exasperation all over him. "I don't even know why I'm bothering to talk to you!"

With that, Adam just stalked away.

8

"My brother, Patrick's, back in town," said Nadine Rivers over the phone. "He wants to talk to you."

"What about?" Diane found it difficult to muster much excitement. Her tiff with Adam had depressed her. Weeks had passed, and the investigation had pretty much hit a dead end.

"About Lynn. He's been thinking about it since the funeral service and I think he's got something that will *prove* that Lynn didn't kill herself!"

She'd liked Patrick when she met him. The idea of new and fresh information to work with was invigorating. Maybe she should go ahead with the investigation, damn the torpedoes.

"It's real simple," said Patrick over a lunch of salad and tuna sandwiches in the Rivers' kitchen. "Just a few short months ago—this summer in fact, my sister renewed her faith in God."

Diane put her uneaten forkful of fresh vegetables back down on her plate. "No *kidding*."

Patrick Rivers was a handsome young man in his early twenties with a shock of black hair and dark, penetrating eyes that seemed to bore into Diane with their honesty and integrity.

"We'd been talking for some time about religious matters—and moral and ethical matters as well," Patrick said in a cleanly enunciated voice that rang with baritone authority—a voice that would sound very good indeed wrapped around a juicy sermon. "After several such dialogues, she came to me and I could see the change in her eyes. They were sparkling eyes now where there had been many clouds before. And she walked taller, as though some weight had been lifted from her shoulders. I asked her what was going on, and she told me, 'Pat, God and I have gotten things right. I think we're on good terms again, and my faith in him has deepened. A lot.' So we knelt right there and then and we prayed together."

"Now tell me, Diane," said Nadine. "Does this sound like a girl who's about to kill herself."

"Lynn knew that suicide is a terrible sin in the eyes of God," said Patrick firmly, his hand clenched with clear emotional conviction. "She would never had killed herself, I'm sure. She could only have been killed, Diane. I promise you that, and I will do whatever I can to help you or the police or whoever to bring this fact into the open—and bring the killer to justice!"

"This is all very well and good," said Diane trying to keep a clear head on the subject. "But you're family, and I don't think that's going to carry much weight with the police. No, we need definite *proof*." She mused on that a moment, toying with her salad, dipping a cut cherry tomato into the vinaigrette dressing and then chewing it thoughtfully. "But something kind of bothers me about this conversion—"

"It wasn't a conversion," corrected Patrick, holding up a teacherlike forefinger in objection. "Call it a 'returning to the fold.' "

"Whatever—you mentioned that Lynn had been acting funny—like she felt guilty about something. . . ."

"I'm not sure if that would be appropriate—"

"Look, if she was killed there may have been more motivation involved than we're aware of, Patrick . . . I know you both loved Lynn, but you've got to come clean here. I mean, if you truly want to find the killer." Diane took a deep, excited breath. "Did Lynn make any kind of confession to you about whatever she felt guilty about?"

"No. She didn't confide or confess anything to me. She just seemed very upset about something. I asked. Believe me, I let her know that whatever it was, she could open up to me." Patrick's dark eyes grew infinitely sad. "But she wouldn't say anything. Maybe it was just too awful . . . but I have the relief of knowing that whatever it was, God has forgiven her."

"Don't you have any idea—any idea whatsoever—what she might have been feeling guilty about? Either one of you?" Diane's frustration was met by silent, unhappy stares.

Finally, Patrick broke the dead air with a soft, introspective voice. "You know, Nadine tells me that you and Lynn were not exactly on the best of terms. She told me about this whole silly gossip business." A sigh. "Ah, human frailties, insecurities—I wish I could say that gossip was the stuff of adoles-

117

cence. Sadly, it even affects places like seminaries. But it really is a minor thing. . . ."

"The gossip that Lynn helped spread hurt a number of people . . . people who might have wanted to hurt her back."

"Yes, so you say. . . . But, surely if you knew her at all you realize that if she was involved with these Evil Sisters, as you call them, it was because she wanted to belong, not because she wanted to hurt anyone."

"That's the reason I'm so dedicated to this investigation, Patrick. I saw that in your sister."

Nadine nodded. "Diane's always tried to get Lynn away from those other girls. . . ."

"She had so many fine, fine qualities," continued Patrick, clearly in a reminiscent mood. "There were things about her that I doubt any of the classmates who criticized her even knew. For example, last year Lynn got involved in helping out an elderly widow, Winifred Jessup. She typed letters for her, filed things, helped her with this and that around the house. All for free, I think. She really did have a good heart. She particularly loved cats and sunny days. . . . But I'm getting maudlin, I guess. It's just that it tortures me that people thought that my sister was somehow bad . . . and bothers me even more that people think she committed suicide."

"This Winifred Jessup . . . maybe she might have some information about Lynn."

"Could be. I think she's in the phone book," said Nadine. "If not, I could probably find her address and phone number for you."

"Okay. Well thank you, Patrick," she said, pushing the rest of her lunch away, her appetite gone.

118

"And thanks for the offer of assistance. Believe me, I'm going to do my best to dig up whatever facts I can—but I'm going to need all the help I can get."

With that she left them.

Diane felt discouraged by her conversation with Patrick and Nadine, which really hadn't provided any new facts. She already had ample reason to believe that Lynn hadn't killed herself—but she needed real evidence. She didn't know where to go with the investigation. And now that she didn't appear to have a boyfriend anymore, everything else seemed kind of gray and depressing. She and Adam hadn't spoken since their argument in his family room. Funny, how when you have someone to hold and kiss, you take him for granted, but when he's gone, you really feel the lack.

Diane, however, was determined to keep on in this pursuit of the killer, without help. And when her work brought the criminal to justice, Adam Grant would be the first person she would see, with a smile on her face and an "I told you so!" on her lips.

Right now, though, the only lead she had was this Winifred Jessup.

Sure enough, the address was in the Maxville phone directory. It was in the Maplewood section, an older part of town. When Diane knocked on the door of the old Edwardian style house, covered with ivy and decked with old iron and wood window boxes filled with plants, an old woman answered.

However, it was not Winifred Jessup.

"I'm sorry, but dear Winnie passed away last year," said the white-haired woman pleasantly, but with a definite frown on her wrinkled face. "God rest her soul."

"Oh. I'm so sorry. . . ."

"You're wondering who I am, no doubt. But then, more importantly, young lady, just who are you?"

Diane explained herself. "I'm trying to meet some of the people who knew Lynn," she finished up.

"Well, you're meeting one right now!" said the woman with a sparkle in her eye. "Nice young girl. But perhaps you'd like a cup of tea."

"That would be very nice, if it's not too much trouble. . . ."

"Oh, no trouble at all. I have some help and we baked a cake just this morning!"

She followed the old lady deep into the house. Diane stepped past an extraordinary number of cats— it seemed as though this woman was a real cat fancier! Still, the place smelled bright and fresh, with no odor of cat boxes.

"But you must forgive me, my dear," said the woman. "My name is Elizabeth Locke. Winifred was my dear friend with whom I played cards and generally kept company. When you're old, my dear, there is nothing nicer than company you don't have to talk to! When Winifred died, she left me her house, along with the charge to take care of her multitude of cats. And so I shall, until my own days dwindle away."

The old lady poured out the tea and offered Diane some very tasty crumpets along with fresh strawberry jam. Diane didn't particularly care to stay here long, but she felt obliged to humor the old lady.

"Thank you, Miss Locke."

"Oh, please call me Betty, everyone calls me

Betty . . . except dear Winifred. . . . She insisted on calling me Elizabeth." The old woman prattled on for a while, pausing only to pet and speak affectionately to her cats.

"Could you tell me something about Winifred and her relationship with Lynn?"

"Hmmm? Lynn. Oh yes, a very sweet, very wonderful girl. Well, as I said, I wasn't here all the time and Lynn only came in a couple of days a week. . . . But she always seemed just a real splendid young lady, and of course Winifred just *doted* on her."

Curious. Lynn's sunny side certainly was showing. Diane listened to a little more of Miss Locke's ramblings, finished her tea and crumpet, and then politely excused herself. "I really must go. So nice to meet you and thank you for the treats, Betty."

As she was being ushered out, however, Diane had a last thought. "By the by . . . I don't mean to pry . . . but just how did Winifred Jessup pass away?"

A cloud passed over Elizabeth Locke's face.

"Poor dear, I suppose life just got to be too much, even with the comforts of her cats and other companionship. One day she apparently decided she couldn't go on. She drew a nice warm bath, took a razor blade and—"

9

There *had* to be a connection.

Winifred Jessup had killed herself in the exact same way that Lynn Rivers had.

The thing was, though, just exactly what *was* that connection? That was the question that stumped Diane. And how could she possibly answer it?

This was the main subject of her thoughts the next day, all the way up to and halfway through chemistry.

Chemistry was when things got a little strange.

Today was lab day. Generally, Diane enjoyed chemistry. Although she was stronger in the softer sciences and less accomplished in stuff like physics, she found that she liked chemistry. Maybe it was just that she liked mixing things together. Anyway, it was all for the best, she thought wryly, since if she decided to pursue criminal investigation rather than journalistic investigation she'd have to take courses in forensics, and chemistry was vital to that area of police procedure.

This week, the lab class was into conversions. Dr. Tankerslee, the teacher, had placed the necessary materials on the lab tables early this morning.

"A common fertilizer, easily enough obtained. And yet, when heated, it becomes something used in dentists' offices. Namely, laughing gas. I want you to collect it, people. *Not* sniff it!" said Dr. Tankerslee, peering over the tops of his half-framed glasses with pixieish enthusiasm, his bushy eyebrows raised high. "Now I want you to take vial number seven and place the contents into the beaker. Put this on the Bunsen burner and connect the tubing to another beaker to collect the gas. The first hint of laughter I hear means there's a leak! First person who collects a significant amount of gas gets a package of Gummi bears!"

This took Diane's mind off her preoccupations. She was interested in this particular game that Mr. Tankerslee was playing so she paid attention. Besides, she loved Gummi bears.

She put the substances Tankerslee had called for in the beaker. She placed the Bunsen burner under an armature and placed the beaker on the armature and made the necessary attachments. Then she lit the burner.

The stuff in the beaker began to heat.

As she waited for the resultant gas to collect, Diane reached over for her pen to mark down any change, and managed to knock the Bic down onto the floor.

"Drat!" she said. She got off her stool and bent over to retrieve it.

Above her, the beaker blew up.

Shards of glass blasted over her, and a heavy cloud of smoke rose up like a smelly omen before the astonished eyes of Dr. Tankerslee and the chemistry class.

"Oh dear," said Dr. Tankerslee, peering up from behind the table where he'd taken refuge. "That was definitely *not* supposed to happen!"

Fortunately, no one was hurt by the explosion.

Dr. Tankerslee, though, insisted on taking Diane to the nurse's office, just to make sure that she was all right. All Diane really needed was a couple of aspirin.

"I can't imagine what happened!" said Dr. Tankerslee, clearly relieved that his student hadn't been harmed. "Someone must have stuck a powdered metal in the mix! A most definite no-no, combining the two."

"Who's your lab assistant?"

"Bob Porter comes in early when I need him."

She found Bob Porter when he came in to do a little work in the lab in his free period. She told the large, owlish boy what had happened. His reaction pretty much told her the story.

He was flabbergasted and surprised and terribly, terribly upset.

No way could this guy have set her up.

"Is there any way that someone could have changed the vial?" she quizzed him.

"Why would anyone want to do that? Are you saying . . . are you saying that someone wanted to hurt you?"

"Or scare me."

"Well, there's about fifteen minutes during homeroom when the lab's empty. Gee, anyone could have come in and planted the vial—we especially label them with students' names, since we don't have the same stuff in every one. . . ."

"You don't?"

"No. We want to mix up the results a bit, to keep you students on your toes. Also to keep things surprising!" A bit of the old enthusiasm and glee crept into Dr. Tankerslee's face.

"It certainly worked that time! It surprised me. Thank heavens I wasn't on my toes."

"Yes, and I am so sorry. . . . We do try to keep things safe in the lab. This kind of business . . . well, it just blows everything." Those bushy eyebrows waggled forlornly. "So to speak."

"Don't worry, Dr. Tankerslee. I think I know why someone did that."

"You're sure it wasn't an accident."

"Positive." She told her teacher the basic story of her theory about Lynn Rivers's death and her subsequent investigation, and the attempts on her life.

"I don't think a small chemical explosion like that could have killed you, although it could have scarred you. Perhaps you should think about curtailing these activities if they are so dangerous."

"Whoever the murderer is, he is definitely trying to get me off the case. I've already promised my parents I'm not investigating anymore, which isn't true. Well, don't worry, Dr. Tankerslee. I believe that my investigation is just about wrapped up."

"You're giving it up then?"

"No. I think I not only have a way to prove that Lynn Rivers did not commit suicide . . ." Diane paused for dramatic effect. "I believe I know the identity of her killer!"

Diane sat behind the wheel of her repaired Toyota and stared hard into the lamplit night. The taste of coffee was bitter in her mouth. She hated coffee, but she knew she was going to have to be totally alert. . . .

And besides, this might be a late night.

Tonight she was going to confront Lynn Rivers's killer.

That morning she had lied to Dr. Tankerslee.

In fact, Diane Delany still had no idea who the killer was. That there was a killer, though, she was sure. The attempts to scare her off the investigation proved that. However, the next attempt—and it seemed inevitable that there would be another—might do more than scare her.

No, she had to crack this case—and fast.

It was getting *very* dangerous. Furthermore, how long would it be before her parents suspected that she wasn't steering clear of the whole matter? Worst of all, she definitely missed Adam—the jerk—and once she showed him she was right, and got this whole thing out of the way, she was certain that they could mend their differences.

No, what she told Dr. Tankerslee was a lie, and she repeated the lie to classmates throughout the day. All she needed to crack the case, she told some school big mouths, was one more bit of evidence. Evidence that she was going to locate that night at Elizabeth Locke's house. Even with the Evil Sisters' swearing off gossip, the rumor mill was still thriving in the halls of Maxville High. How long would it be before the news got back to the killer?

She was banking on its being soon enough for him to be here tonight.

Fall was edging toward winter, and the air had gone cold. What little warmth that the Toyota's heater had generated had long since dissipated. The only thing that kept Diane sort of warm was her long down winter coat.

She shivered. Her breath was starting to mist.

She sipped from the Thermos of coffee and watched the door of the house that had once belonged to Winifred Jessup.

Her plan was pretty simple. She was counting on the killer coming to the house to try to stop her. Even if he suspected a trap, he couldn't take the chance that there *was* some evidence at Mrs. Locke's house pointing to him. All Diane had to do was wait in her car, parked discreetly in the alley across the way, and wait to see who showed up.

She'd checked with Elizabeth Locke, of course, and relayed her suspicions. Mrs. Locke had been happy to help bring a criminal to justice, especially if that criminal had possibly harmed Winnie Jessup. She had promised not to answer the door to anyone. This would give Diane plenty of time to check on the identity of the person who showed up.

And show up he would, Diane felt that in her bones.

The trap had been set. All she had to do now was wait.

And pray that the killer wouldn't get her indirectly by making her wait too long out here and freezing her butt off!

Diane sipped at the coffee again, more for the heat than the caffeine, and was wondering just how long she was going to be able to do this, when a young man strode past the entry to the alley.

He was walking so quickly that she didn't have a

chance to see who it was as he sailed right on up the steps to the door of the old house.

Who was he? She cursed her coffee break. She should have been watching! She'd missed her chance to identify him as he passed her car and he was wearing the collar of his overcoat up so that it hid his face.

The guy knocked on the door.

There was no getting around it. She was going to have to get out of the car, go up, and get a better look.

She opened the door as quietly as she could and slid out onto the pavement. She'd worn her tennis shoes, so she was able to dash across the street and then sneak up to the side of the stairs and peer up through the narrow slits in the railing without being seen.

It was a young man, and he looked very annoyed that his knocking was not being answered.

Diane caught her breath, astonished at the identity of the person who surely must be Lynn Rivers's killer.

For standing at the front door of Elizabeth Locke's house was Adam Grant!

10

Adam!

Panic stirred at the base of Diane's spine. She had to clamp a hand over her mouth to muffle the yelp of surprise that threatened.

Adam Grant!

How could he possibly be a murderer!

She could feel herself getting faint and she stepped back to regain her balance, stepping on a piece of loose rock.

It skittered away, making a slight noise.

Adam swiveled around, looking nervous. "Who's that!"

Diane flung herself against the side of the steps, crouching down to make sure she was swallowed up by the shadows.

"Is there anyone there?" Adam asked again. "Shoot," he said, looking back at the door. "No one home. Strange . . ."

Diane listened with vast relief as his footsteps retreated into the distance.

When she felt it was safe, she let out a gasp of relief.

But it wasn't really relief she felt . . . more than anything, she felt confusion.

Adam . . . the murderer? It didn't make sense. But she still didn't have all the facts. And some of the facts she did have could point to Adam. Adam had insisted that Lynn's death was a suicide . . . he'd argued with her to stop her investigation. . . .

And that guy driving by Lynn's house . . . maybe it wasn't Jim at all. . . . Maybe it was Adam. . . .

Adam was certainly strong enough to hold Lynn down without showing signs of struggle. . . . The autopsy had shown no drugs in her system, so that must have been the way he'd done it. . . .

No. Hold it. There was no proof here . . . and no motive.

This was Adam Grant . . . someone that she had cared about . . . no, *did* care about.

She should have confronted him when she first saw him. She had to find out the truth . . . right now.

Bracing herself, she pushed out from the shadows and down the street.

She glimpsed Adam, turning at the corner, being swallowed from sight by a large stone wall. Hastily, she followed. She had to talk to him . . . she had to give him a chance before she went to the police and implicated him in the murder of Lynn Rivers!

The cold forgotten, her coat flapping about her legs, Diane ran for all she was worth, barely slowing down to negotiate the corner. The sight that met her eyes, however, brought her up short.

The lamplit street was empty.

Absolutely no sign of anyone.

Where could he have gone to? Frustration welled up inside her.

She was about to turn around and head back to her car when someone leapt out from behind the bushes and grabbed her from behind. An arm was flung around her neck, choking her. From the corner of her eye, startled, she saw a knife flash.

Its cold edge pressed against her throat.

"Okay, don't move and I won't hurt you. . . . What are you doing here and why did—" said Adam, and then he stopped in mid sentence. "Oh—God . . . it's you!"

Immediately he released her.

She spun about, staring in disbelief at the knife. It was just a dull Boy Scout knife.

"Oh, this," said Adam. "It was . . . well, it was just to scare the—"

"Adam," she said, warily backing away from him, ready to bolt and run for her life. "Why did you kill her, Adam?"

She wasn't really convinced that he *had* killed Lynn, but she thought that by confronting him with the possibility, maybe she'd get the truth.

"Kill? What are you talking about?" He looked honestly baffled. "I didn't kill anyone!"

She wanted to believe him. "Then what are you doing here, knocking at Elizabeth Locke's door—falling right into my trap for the killer?"

His mouth dropped. "You think that . . . Look, Sherlock Delany . . . things are not that elementary. . . . What, you think I didn't hear about what you were saying at school? You think I didn't figure out this silly little trap of yours? Diane . . . I

131

saw trouble coming here, big trouble, and I came to protect you!''

"Protect me! With a pocketknife!"

"Look, if I'd wanted to kill you, I'd have come a little more heavily armed than this!"

She had to agree that what he was saying made sense.

Besides, as they stood there facing each other, as he stepped toward her, entreatingly, she remembered all the kind things he had done for her, the gentleness he'd shown her, the vulnerability. . . .

Despite his sometimes jerky behavior, he really was a sweetheart. He couldn't be a murderer.

"You know," he continued, "I'm kinda upset that you'd think I could do this kind of thing! I thought you knew me better than that. You've got no reason to suspect me . . . really.'' He looked thoughtful for a moment. "Listen . . . it's pretty certain that whoever's been hassling you is going to buy your bait tonight and show up. When he shows up, you'll see it wasn't me.''

She sighed. "Okay. I guess maybe you're right. But we don't stick together. I could use someone to cover the back of the house. That's your job, okay?''

"Right. Have you found anything else out . . . any other clues?''

She told him about the whole business with Winifred Jessup and Lynn Rivers, and about Elizabeth Locke's cooperation with her scheme.

"So that's why she didn't answer the door.''

"Right, and she's not going to. Anyone who comes to the front door, I'll see. And now you'll be covering the back door.''

As she headed back to her hiding place in her car,

she felt much better about everything. Adam was less and less a suspect in her mind, and she was more and more certain that the killer would oblige them by showing up at the old Jessup house. And her renewed faith in Adam made her feel a lot safer.

She got in her car, sipped cooling coffee, and waited.

Yes, that was something that she'd always wanted from Adam. A little support, someone to help her out. And now that she had it, she felt *much* better, much more secure.

Yes, she thought, shivering behind the steering wheel, as she once more watched the front door of the old house. It's scary to be alone and facing grown-up problems all of a sudden when just a few short weeks ago you were a typical high school student. She'd be more than happy to get back to her familiar old teenage anxieties and problems once this whole thing was *over!*

She waited.

And she waited some more.

"C'mon, guy!" she said, looking at her watch, wondering how long she'd be able to hold out before she either had to turn on the engine and the heater or give up on this whole thing entirely. The colder she got, the more foolish it seemed. If the killer hadn't gotten the message that Adam had, then maybe she'd somehow missed the mark. . . .

Her chilling mind was mulling this possibility over when the unexpected happened.

A gunshot sounded from inside the house!

Even from here, though muffled by distance and brick and metal and glass, she could hear the cold abrupt snap of the explosion and she knew instinctively that it wasn't a car backfiring.

She sat still for a moment, her heart beating rapidly.

Mrs. Locke!

She got out of her car and raced to the front door. Locked, of course. Foolish of her. She hadn't seen anyone go in or come out. And she didn't have a key.

The backdoor was the only possibility.

She hurried around to the back of the house. There was a spacious yard, with a large old-fashioned back porch, complete with a hanging plant holder, a wicker table and rocking chairs. Where was Adam?

The old oak door gaped open. Mrs. Locke's cats had escaped into the yard, and Diane wondered why the old lady wasn't outside rounding them up.

She ran inside. All the house was dark save for a light in the parlor.

A funny smell permeated the house. A garage-type smell that she couldn't identify.

Diane went into the next room.

In the middle of the room, lying on the floor and oozing blood from her chest, was the body of Elizabeth Locke.

And standing over her, holding a gun, was Adam Grant.

11

"Diane!" said Adam, looking up at her. The gun wasn't smoking, but it might as well have been. "This isn't how it looks!"

He tossed the gun down in front of her as though it had suddenly turned white hot.

Diane could only stare at the tableau before her with shock and horror. Adam Grant, standing over the body of that poor old lady, blood dripping from a hole in her chest. She went to her and felt for a pulse. Nothing.

"Mrs. Locke!" she gasped. "You killed Mrs. Locke!"

"No! I heard the shot, just like you did. I rushed in here, and I saw this old lady lying here. . . . I came over, and I picked up the gun, and that's how you found me. . . . Honest to God . . . please believe me!" There was a desperate look on Adam's face that she couldn't interpret. Had he been telling the truth about everything from the beginning or had it all been nothing but lies?

But another question rose up in her mind. *Motive.*

Why?

Why would Adam kill Lynn Rivers?

Why should he kill Mrs. Locke?

Still, it looked pretty bad, and Diane didn't want to take any chances.

She stepped forward, leaned over, and scooped up the gun. Putting her hand on the trigger, she raised the gun and pointed it at Adam. "Don't move! I don't want you to come anywhere near me, Adam!"

"But Diane, I swear, I didn't kill anybody!"

"I'm not saying you did. I just don't want to take any chances this time, Adam!"

Adam looked as terrified now as she was. For a moment there was a deadlock, fear permeating the air with its stink of tension. . . .

And then from outside footsteps sounded.

Footsteps? thought Diane. Who could it be? She prayed it was the police. . . .

But it wasn't.

She turned her head to see Melissa Birch and Toni Ayers walking hesitantly into the parlor.

What were they doing here?

"Are you okay, Diane?" Melissa asked.

"Oh my God!" said Toni, staring aghast at the body. "Mrs. Locke." She looked up at Adam. "You shot her, Adam!"

"I did not shoot her!"

"Keep the gun trained on him," Toni said. "I never trusted Adam Grant, but I didn't think that he was a killer!"

"I'm nothing of the sort!"

"Where did you come from?" asked Diane.

"We were just driving past in Toni's car," said

Melissa. "We were wondering if maybe you might need some help."

"We'd pretty much figured out what you were doing," Toni continued, "and we thought you might have gotten yourself into trouble here. Boy, we were right more than we realized."

"We heard a shot!" said Melissa excitedly. "And we saw you rushing to the backyard!"

"And we came in to help out!"

"Don't listen to them, Diane," said Adam, losing his imploring tone and starting to sound desperate. "They're lying!"

Diane ignored him. "Did you call the police first?" she asked the girls.

"No, but we'll do it right now. Just keep the gun on this murderer here!" said Melissa. "Keep him covered. You know, I kind of always suspected that if you were right and Lynn didn't commit suicide, then Adam Grant was the one who killed her."

Toni looked down at Mrs. Locke's body and shuddered. "This certainly proves it, doesn't it?"

Diane was more confused than ever. Nothing made sense anymore. Had she been dating a murderer? Was Adam Grant truly capable of such a thing?

A single question, however, kept Diane hovering on the brink, preventing her from simply accepting Toni's word on the matter.

"But *why?*"

The words came from her mouth tremulously, almost defensively, as though she were a lawyer who'd just had her case pulled from beneath her like a rug.

A kind of knowing look crept over Toni's features and a snide smile touched her lips. "You know, it's funny. Me and my yapping mouth . . . well, you're well aware of my love of gossip, Diane. But the one time I showed some restraint, perhaps I shouldn't have. Things might never have come to this."

"What are you talking about?"

"Yeah. Just what *are* you talking about?" Adam said, stepping forward.

"Get back!" Diane warned him, nervously waving the gun.

"Remember that day a while back, when there was something I had to tell you—but didn't?"

"Yes . . . I suppose so. But what does that have to do with Adam?" asked Diane, beginning to dread hearing what Toni was about to reveal.

"Everything. What I was about to tell you was about Lynn and Adam here." She took a deep breath and then frowned at Adam. "I'm surprised he didn't tell you. . . ."

"Didn't tell me what, Adam?"

Melissa blurted out the rest, unable to stand the suspense. "They used to go out! Adam and Lynn!"

"But only for a while . . ." said Toni. "We heard the whole sad story from Lynn. This jerk dated her for a while, but he only had one thing on his mind."

"Yeah," said Melissa, sneering. "And you can probably figure out what it was, having dated this sex maniac yourself."

"Adam!" Diane said, struggling to keep the gun steady.

"That's nonsense."

"You deny you went out with her?" snapped Toni.

"No, but—"

"But *nothing*. Lynn told us all about it. You just

138

kept on pushing and pushing, and then when you finally got what you wanted, you just *dumped* her. She wasn't good enough for you anymore; you wanted to prove your irresistible charms with a tougher victim, like Diane here. But I guess Diane's not quite so easy to persuade as poor Lynn. So you got horny and you went back for more from Lynn that Sunday . . . but she'd learned her lesson and refused. . . . So you got really psycho—and you killed her! You murdered her!''

Diane was struck dumb by Toni's story. It didn't seem possible, but Adam *was* sometimes a bit much to handle. And why had he never told her about dating Lynn?

"This is absurd," Adam said, looking helpless and frightened. "I—I *did* go out with Lynn for a few weeks. But this business about—sex and getting my way . . . well, that's absolutely not true! Diane . . . you know me . . . you know how I am. . . . I've never been that way with you. . . . I mean—"

She cut him off. "You didn't tell me about her. Why didn't you tell me you dated her . . . ?"

"I . . . well . . . Diane, I thought you *knew*. It's just not something you talk about with girlfriends. . . . It made me feel . . . I don't know. I thought since you didn't like them . . ."

Toni glowered at him. "But you admit, you not only dated her, you dated her steadily. I mean, you guys were a couple. You were all over each other!"

"We liked each other, yeah. Yeah, and I guess maybe it was kinda, well, physical. But this was before we got together, Diane," Adam said firmly, his voice gaining authority and conviction. "And we broke off, yeah—but it wasn't because of the reason they said. No, Diane, we broke up because of these two foul snakes here!"

"Us! That's utter nonsense," said Melissa. "You broke up with her for the reasons Toni said."

"No way, sister." He turned back to Diane and spoke clearly and plainly, enunciating his words carefully to make sure that she understood each one. "Like I said, Diane. Lynn and I dated, yes. But we broke up because of Melissa Birch and Toni Ayers. Lynn was trying to change the direction her life was taking; she realized that the kind of things she was indulging in with the Evil Sisters was very wrong, very harmful—"

"Oh, spare us the sermonizing," said Toni, sneering.

"No, Toni. Let him have his say," said Diane, keeping the gun steady, keeping her voice calm, cold, and in control. "He deserves a chance too."

"Thank you, Diane. Lynn was coming to realize that these two witches were a bad influence on her, and she was trying not to socialize with them—but it was really odd. They . . . well, they had some kind of hold on her. I don't know what it was. We would make a date, and then she would cancel it with a really silly excuse. And I would press her, and she would say that she was busy with something. Well, I got jealous one of those times. . . . I thought maybe she was seeing some other guy. Hey, I'm human. So I followed her. And you know where she was going . . . I wish it was to another guy! No, it was to Toni Ayers's house. When I confronted her and asked her why Toni and Melissa had such a hold on her, she wouldn't say. What she told me, crying, was that she had to do whatever they told her to!"

"Rubbish!" Toni interjected.

"And you know what she told me they'd told her that night? They told her that she couldn't see me anymore. She told me that we had to break up!"

"Now why—"

"And *that's* why we broke up. Not because I wanted to . . . but because they somehow got between us," Adam finished, looking sad.

"What about all those fights you had with Lynn!" said Melissa. "We were worried about her! You were getting absolutely violent. We were really concerned about her safety. We didn't have any hold on her—"

"Lies! Total lies, Diane!"

"And there was something else weird going on there too," said Toni. "We don't know what it was, but it had something to do with Winifred Jessup."

"We think that he was blackmailing her," added Toni.

"That's enough!" Red faced, Adam started toward Melissa, hands outstretched as though to grab her and wring her neck.

"Stay right where you are!" cried Diane. She waved the gun and brought Adam up short. Apparently for a moment he'd forgotten she was pointing the thing at him.

"Step back!"

Adam did so. "Think about this, Diane. Think about them and think about me! Now who are you going to trust!"

She wanted to trust Adam, there was no question about that. And, God knows, the Evil Sisters were famous for lying. But at least part of their story rang true. One of the problems she always had about

Adam was that simple necking wasn't enough. When they got along and started kissing, he wanted more than Diane was prepared to give him. And he was very, very insistent sometimes! She could well see a girl weaker than herself giving in. But would he *murder* someone over sex?

Suddenly Diane was tired, too tired to think. This was too much for her to figure out on her own. This was something that should be turned over to the police to decide.

Regardless of what had happened to Lynn, Elizabeth Locke had been murdered. And when it came to murder, *they* were the experts, not her.

"I'm sorry, Adam, but this is all too much for me." She turned to the girls. "Call the police, will you?"

"Sure," said Melissa, starting away.

Toni grabbed her, halting her. "Wait a minute, Mel. The police are going to want a lot of details." She turned to Diane. "You're the one who saw things here first, you're the one who can explain a lot more to them—stuff they'll want right away!"

Diane was hardly listening. She was too stunned and upset by the look of outrage and anger—and yes, betrayal, on Adam's face.

No, she didn't really know the guy.

Not at all.

"Okay, cover him," she said, absently handing the gun over to Toni, who took it readily and maintained the aim on Adam.

She went toward the door to look for the phone.

But Melissa stepped around and stood directly in her pathway. "Uh, uh, sweetheart, I don't think that would be a good idea."

"What?"

"She's right, you know," Toni's voice came from behind.

Diane Delany whirled around.

Toni Ayers was smiling.

And aiming the gun right at her!

12

Diane felt as though she'd been hit over the head by a sledgehammer.

Toni Ayers had stepped back a few paces, in order to be able to cover both Adam and Diane. Her face had changed entirely from the mask of innocent self-righteousness to one of hatred, maliciousness—and just a smidgen of fear. All the stress she'd been feeling before translated into a slightly nervous shaking of her hands and a tic in her face.

Unfortunately it did not affect her hold on the gun—or that weapon's deadliness. And clearly she was not afraid to use it. The crazed look in Toni's eyes told Diane who was capable of pulling the trigger on Elizabeth Locke.

"Oh, Adam, I'm so sorry I didn't believe you."

"Save it. Right now we have to deal with the present." He turned to Toni. "I figured that story about driving by was nonsense. You must have shot her, then run upstairs and hid. So when I came in, and Diane followed, you made your grand entry, with the story you'd concocted upstairs."

"Thought you were so smart, huh? And you too, Diane!" Melissa snickered.

"Miss Sherlock and her faithful assistant, Dr. Stupid!" Toni giggled.

Diane realized the truth in a flash.

"It all fits now. . . . You two killed your own friend! *You* murdered Lynn Rivers!"

"Big surprise," said Adam sarcastically. "Weren't you listening to me, Diane? I suspected as much. But I'd already learned my lesson. I'd been burned by these two. And since there was absolutely no way of proving anything about Lynn, I just let the whole matter lie where it was. Well, I guess I'm paying for my cowardice now. Maybe if I'd said something, Elizabeth Locke would be alive, and we wouldn't be here now."

"That's why you didn't want me to get involved," said Diane.

"Yeah. I figured it might be black widow deadly. Looks like I was all too correct, huh?" He looked down to Elizabeth Locke's body. "I still can't get the connection, though. That's what bothers me. I mean, I knew that Lynn had worked for Winifred Jessup last year—she told me that much—"

"They must have murdered her as well!" said Diane. "Mrs. Locke told me that Winifred Jessup died in the exact same way as Lynn—in a bathtub, after slitting her wrists. Seemingly a suicide."

Adam glared at Toni and Melissa. "I just can't figure out how everything fits together."

"Huh," Melissa snorted contemptuously. "Why should we spill the beans now?"

Toni chuckled throatily. "What difference does it make, Melissa?"

Melissa nodded. "Well, maybe you're right."

"What are you talking about?" said Diane.

Toni motioned with the gun. "You'll see. Come on. Both of you. Let's start climbing those stairs. We're going to make a little visit to the top floor!"

Her face was filled with a horrible and quite frightening combination of sadistic pleasure and anticipation.

It was the biggest bathroom that Diane had ever seen.

A Victorian bathroom, it seemed to stretch on forever, an ocean of tile and ceramic. It smelled of lavender and Pear's soap and talcum powder. Shelves along the floral print wallpaper were stacked with tasseled towels and colorful bric-a-brac. The handles on the sink faucets and the top of the old-fashioned top flush commode were made of brightly polished wood.

It was a cold and awful place to die.

The first thing that Diane noticed, though, was the bathtub.

It was an old-fashioned bathtub, spacious as the lifeboat of a yacht. It had no shower fixtures, no curtain, and its porcelain was as white as ivory and shiny, as though it had just been scrubbed and Ajaxed and then wiped clean. Its feet were large and scrolled.

The strangest thing about this bathtub, however, was its position in the room.

Unlike most bathtubs, it wasn't installed against the wall. Rather, it pointed out toward the middle of the vast expanse of tile as though set adrift.

This, Diane knew without having to ask, was the bathtub in which Winifred Jessup had died.

And she knew also that Toni and Melissa planned the identical fate for her and Adam.

Adam seemed to sense this as well.

As soon as he walked into the cold expanse of the room after Melissa had clicked on the overhead light, he spun around and confronted the gun-pointing Toni.

"You're *not* going to get away with this!" he said, anger covering any fear he felt.

"Get away with what?"

"What you did to Winifred Jessup. Right here in this very same room!"

"No, you don't understand. *We* didn't do anything to dear Winnie. Right, Melissa?"

Melissa nodded. "Oh no. That was definitely Lynn. Lynn was the one who did that."

"Nonsense! I knew Lynn, and she'd never be involved in a murder!" Adam's indignation caused his face to turn red.

"But she was," said Melissa.

"Oh, it doesn't make any difference anymore," said Toni. "They're not going to be able to tell anyone anyway."

"Tell what?" said Adam. "Go ahead. I for one want to know the truth."

At this point, Diane didn't want to know anything except how she was going to get *away* from this awful bathroom.

"Uh, uh," said Toni. "First things first. I want you two to strip down to your underwear. Melissa, you got the stuff?"

"Yes, it's over in that medicine cabinet."

"Good. Get it."

Toni stepped over to the tub.

Keeping the gun leveled on Diane and Adam, she leaned over, took the rubber stopper perched on the

147

side of the tub, and stuck it down onto the plug hole. Then she turned on the hot water knob and let the water cascade, steaming, into the vast tub.

It made a drumming, scary, hollow sound.

Toni tested it. "Ouch. Much too hot. Let's put a little *C* into the mix." She twisted the appropriate knob, then she checked the water again. "Ah. Much better."

"Just what was going on with Winifred Jessup, anyway?" said Adam, his eye trained upon the revolver as though waiting for the slightest opportunity to wrest it from Toni's grasp.

"Actually, it was truly Lynn who started that little number. She needed a little extra money so she answered an ad in the paper for a part-time private secretary. The cheap old biddy Jessup took her on because she was a minor and she could pay her peanuts. At first we thought it was really stupid for Lynn to work for Winifred Jessup, but then we changed our minds. Right, Melissa dear?"

"Whatever you say," said the tall girl, coming back with a leather case and handing it to Toni. She didn't look pleased that this story was reaching anyone's ears.

"I can't do anything with this with a gun in my hand, silly. Open it up. Show our guests what we've got for them!"

Melissa nodded. She unzipped the leather case, pulling out the contents. Even though she knew what to expect, Diane had to gasp when she saw what Melissa pulled out, glittering in the electric light.

The antique straight razor was scalpel sharp.

13

"You think that you're going to get away with this for the third time in a row!" said Adam, shocked as much with disbelief as with fear at the sight of the deadly instrument, gleaming evilly in Melissa's hand.

Diane could smell her own fear and sweat seeping into the sterile, clean bathroom.

Toni smiled slyly. "And why not? Look, there's a dead body down there with a bullet in its chest, and someone is going to have to take the rap. Why not the people who committed the other murders—and in the exact same manner?"

"That's really stupid, Toni. I mean, really dumb!"

"Just shut up!" the girl yelled. She took a couple of steps, moving closer to Adam, her finger tightening on the trigger. "You want to get your head blown off, huh?"

She was crazy.

The girl had to be crazy! There was no point in trying to reason with her.

"No! No, he doesn't! Just let us go, Toni. Let us go, and we'll forget about this whole thing."

"That's pretty hard to do with a dead body down there. No, we're going to have to have scapegoats. How convenient that you two are here! So nice of you to drop in!"

"You still haven't explained why you shot that poor old woman. You never finished the story of Lynn and Mrs. Jessup."

"And you haven't done what I told you to. I'll make a deal with you. Start taking off those clothes—slowly!—and each button unbuttoned, each zipper undone, I'll give you another juicy bit of some *real* gossip."

So as Diane slowly and reluctantly took off first her coat and then her shoes, Toni Ayers wove her incredible tale.

The odd thing was that the relationship of the Evil Sisters had been, at least partly, financial from the very beginning. Even back as far as third grade, Toni and Melissa had been drawn to Lynn by the money she always had. While all three girls were from well-to-do families, only Lynn had parents who were generous to their daughter.

What Lynn needed, the others rapidly realized, was attention and most of all a sense of belonging. So they fashioned their own exclusive club of three, which they would occasionally expand to include other girls, who generally remained only long enough to lose dolls, money, and other possessions.

With puberty came a change of priorities. But if anything, the girls got worse, learning the power of words and rumor to control the social byways of junior high and high school. However, they also learned that being "superior" meant you had to dress that way, and that cost money.

Unfortunately, their fathers still gave them paltry allowances, which meant they had to find other ways of getting money to buy the right stuff.

"That's how we got into finding out stuff about people," said Toni. "We figured a few years ago that all these things we were discovering about people were powerful in many ways—not just for gossip."

Diane nodded. "I suspected as much. When you had a really good story on someone, you blackmailed them, didn't you!"

"Hey, dressing like teenaged goddesses costs hard cold cash!" said Melissa, looking proud of herself.

"We had to find some way of getting the things we needed," said Toni without a trace of apology or regret in her voice. "So anyway, when Lynn got the job with Miss Jessup we discovered that she definitely had resources she didn't talk much about."

"A miser. Just like our fathers!" said Melissa. "It didn't take much homework to discover that the lady was loaded. So we figured this lady wouldn't miss much of her pile, if we siphoned off some of it cleverly."

Toni and Melissa had discovered that in addition to the usual filing, letter writing, dictation, and other odd jobs, Lynn would also pay bills for the dim-sighted Winifred Jessup. Each week she would present the older woman with filled-out checks and guide her hand to the signature line, on which Miss Jessup would simply scribble her name trustingly, without question.

"So it was quite simple, really," said Toni. "We

just had her write out fifty dollar checks each week to me. Lynn would burn the stubs. When the canceled checks came back, she got rid of those too. It was a perfect source of cash.''

"Embezzlement," said Adam, now out of his shoes and down to his jockey shorts. "But something must have gone wrong—so it wasn't so perfect.''

"It would have been perfect if Lynn hadn't screwed up and forgotten to destroy one of the canceled checks. Miss Jessup happened to have a magnifying glass available and she saw who they were written to. She would never have guessed! The old lady had plenty of money. . . . She would have died a natural death without being any the wiser. . . .''

Diane had stopped, just before removing her jeans. "But she didn't die a natural death, did she?''

"I think you know the answer to that.''

"So that's it," Adam said. "That's why Lynn was suffering all those pangs of guilt.''

"Yeah," said Melissa. "She was the one who thought up the way Mrs. J. should croak.''

"She pointed out that the old woman had been real depressed because one of her cats had died recently. She was depressed and everyone knew it.''

"Yeah, so we just drew the water and held the old lady down. Lynn did the cutting.''

"No," shouted Adam. "I don't believe that. Lynn would never do something like that.''

"You'd be surprised.''

Diane agreed with Adam, but she said nothing. What good would it do? What she'd figured out though was probably a lot closer to the truth.

Lynn had probably balked very early in the situation. But the other Sisters really had something on her now, and forced her to continue the tap of Winifred Jessup's resources. No *way* could Lynn have been involved physically in Mrs. Jessup's murder. But then again, she wouldn't have been able to run to the police either. Lynn was implicated in the whole scheme.

This was why she'd been acting so strangely.

And, most certainly, this was why she'd tried to reform—and why she hadn't been able to.

She could imagine what the Sisters had told her! "Lynn, babe, you go to the police with the truth, and it will be child's play to make sure you take the rap!" She could almost hear Melissa's tough-toned voice. "You're the one who was working for her. We're just people that you hang out with and we can dump you—" snap of fingers "—like that. And where will you be then—nobody will like you then. You won't have anybody. You're nobody without us!"

And that, of course, Diane realized, was the key to the whole sick relationship.

"So you found out she was going to the police." Adam interrupted her thoughts. "You couldn't afford that, and by now it was too late to declare your own innocence in the matter. You knew that she would be alone that Sunday. You had to stop her from going to the police. You went to her house and had a confrontation. She stood up to you. You pulled this gun. And then you did to her what you did to Mrs. Jessup."

"My goodness, how clever," said Toni. "You've figured it all out! You get an *A* for logical reasoning. Yes, that's right. Lynn had deserted us. She wasn't playing the game anymore, so we had to get rid of her. But you know, it wasn't painful. In fact, it was very peaceful. Cutting your wrists in a warm bath is a very peaceful, relaxed way to die. It's the way I'd go. Maybe it's the way I will go—when I'm about ninety!''

"Let us go," said Diane. "You can't keep on this path, Toni. It will catch up with you eventually.''

"You're not going to be able to stop me, though. Now step into the tub.''

"No!''

"Do it!'' snarled Toni, waving the gun. "Do it now!''

Diane was down to her underwear now.

All this time, she'd hoped that stalling would give someone else time to arrive. She'd prayed that another person down the road had perhaps heard the shot and had called the police.

Apparently, though, no one had.

She stepped into the tub.

Melissa handed her the razor. "Here you go, dearie. A present. I believe you know what to do with it!''

14

"No!" cried Adam.

"Please," said Diane in a small, terrified voice. "Don't make me do this."

"If you don't," said Toni, stepping forward and pointing the gun toward Adam's temple, "I shall be quite happy to pull this trigger and splatter your boyfriend's—excuse me, *ex* but-you-still-love-him boyfriend's—brains all over this bathroom! Do you really want to see that? I should think it would be rather like something out of a *Living Dead* zombie movie, with very *red* special effects." Toni's eyes got even more wild and crazed. "You know, I'm almost tempted to pull the trigger just to see what it looks like—never saw anyone's brains blast out of his skull, have you? We could just say that *you* did it, Diane? A spurned lover's revenge."

My God! She really was crazy!

"No!" cried Adam.

"Then I'll tell you what I want you to do." Toni's eyes seemed to glitter with excitement. "I want you to sit down and relax in that nice hot tub. Then I want you to take that razor that dear Melissa has gifted you with and I want you to just make a little line across your wrist and put it in the water and then just relaaaaaaaaaaax! All your problems will be over!''

"Yeah," said Melissa. "And everything will be peaceful and you won't have to worry about anything!''

"No!" repeated Adam. "Don't, Diane! I love you! Please don't do it!''

"Well, well, well! Isn't this lovely!" said Toni. "The lover professes!''

"Drama!" said Melissa.

"No, pure melodrama. Now keep your mouth shut or I'll put a bullet through it, Grant!''

"Don't," said Diane. "I'll get in.''

She stepped into the tub. The water was hot, but not uncomfortably so. She pulled her other leg in and then stood there, holding the razor uncertainly above her bare arm.

"Sit down!''

She sat down, letting the steamy water close up over her body.

She felt as though she was settling down into her own grave.

"Excellent. Now, the wrist, Diane. The wrist, or I'll pull this trigger, I swear to God I will.''

Diane pulled her arm down and looked at her bare wrist, suddenly aware of her pulse hammering in her forehead, flowing through that blue squiggle that was the vein below her pale skin.

She had to stall.

But how?

She had a sudden idea.

"Toni. I don't—''

"What's the problem now?''

"I don't know . . . I don't know where to cut."

"That's nonsense. Just across the wrist."

"No really. I mean, the best place!"

"There is no best place."

"You don't want me to die?"

"What do you mean?"

"I mean, if I don't cut in the right place I might just pass out. I've heard of that happening, haven't you? I could just konk out and when I'm discovered, I'd tell them all about you!"

"You're really something, you know!"

"Also, I don't want to hurt."

"Just put the blade on the wrist."

Diane put the sharp edge of the razor blade onto the palm of her hand. "Here?"

"No! Stupid, that's not your wrist! Up! Further up!"

Diane pulled the blade a full eight inches up her forearm. "You mean up here?"

"What are you, Diane, an idiot?" said Toni. "Are you going to make me do it myself?"

"If you just show me where, I'll give it a try."

"Oh, honestly!"

Taking her attention off Adam and shaking her head with total vexation, Toni stepped forward, pointing her free finger and giving specific instructions.

"Right across there, Diane. Make it long and make it deep and everything will be—"

"NOOOOOOOOOOOOOOOOOOOOOOOOO!"

The scream was something out of a horror movie, complete with special sound reverb. It was so loud and so startling that even the seemingly iron-nerved Toni was affected.

She froze and looked over to where it came from.

It was Adam, screaming. He was stepping forward, arms stretched toward Toni, his face contorted like a madman's.

Melissa rushed forward to stop him and they collided hard like a couple of wrestlers in a ring.

Toni started to swing the gun around. But it didn't make it all the way.

For Diane, seeing her chance, acted. With a waving rush of water, she pushed forward, reached out, and *grabbed* Toni by the wrist, and *yanked* as hard as she could.

Toni, taken totally by surprise, lost her balance and was pulled back like a marionette on a string. All of her weight was focused on her backward spin, and she hurled backward, sprawling across the rim of the bathtub.

With a great splash and scream, Toni Ayers rammed her head against the side of the great bathtub!

15

Toni groaned and fell to the floor, unconscious.

The gun slipped from her hand and fell into the tub of water.

"Toni!" screamed Melissa.

With a surprising show of force, Melissa broke free from Adam's hold. She jumped for the tub and plunged her hands in the water, scrabbling for the gun.

Diane punched her in the face.

Spurting blood from her nose, Melissa fell back onto the floor.

"Diane! Are you okay?" Adam said.

Diane threw the razor onto the floor and pushed herself up and out from the hateful bathtub. "Yes."

"Toni's down for the count."

"We have to get Melissa."

But Melissa had already sprung up from her tumble. Instead of coming back to her friend's aid, though, once she was back on her feet, she sprinted out the door. A moment later, Diane heard the clatter of feet down the stairs.

"Come on! We've got to get her before she gets away!" shouted Diane.

"You're all wet!"

"Don't worry about me, Adam. GO AND GET HER!"

Adam ignored her. Upon a hook was an old red bathrobe. He grabbed this and put it over Diane's shoulders. "I'm so glad you're okay."

"I won't be okay until these girls are locked up."

"Okay. C'mon, let's get Melissa. I can run faster than her any day of the week. Don't worry, we'll catch her."

"Not if we stand here yapping."

"Good point."

Adam sprinted out before her, and he was right; he ran fast. By the time Diane had made it to the end of the landing, he was more than halfway down the stairs. He took the final dozen or so in one Herculean leap, bounding up from a squat in the blink of an eye and then running into the parlor.

Halfway down the steps, she smelled that funny smell again.

It wasn't until she reached the bottom that she realized what it was.

Gasoline!

What was a gasoline smell doing in a house?

She didn't stop to consider, she just hauled on after Adam into the parlor.

The sight that met her eyes there brought her up short.

There was Adam Grant, standing stock-still, a horrified expression on his face.

In front of him was Melissa Birch holding a large

can of gasoline, spilling the last bit out onto the rug and a couch, a maniacal expression on her face.

"Okay, you stop there too!" said Melissa. "You just don't *take another step!*" She produced a box of kitchen matches from a pocket, pulled out a long red-and-white-tipped match and *FWICK!* suddenly there was a light on the end. " 'Cause if you do I'm going to light this couch, and this whole house will go up in *flames!*"

Fire!

Her deepest fear gripped her.

Gasping, she stepped back.

"I said *don't move!*" Melissa yelled again.

"Just stay where you are, Diane," said Adam. "She's poured out that gas can and another one all over the house. They must have brought them over when they came to see Mrs. Locke."

"But . . . why?"

"Why do you think? To destroy the evidence! We knew there was the chance that Mrs. Locke wouldn't know about it or wouldn't tell us about it—so we figured this was the one sure way of destroying it."

"Evidence?" said Diane.

"The evidence that was supposed to attract the killer," said Adam. "Don't you remember, Diane?"

"But . . . but that doesn't exist!"

"What?" Melissa's broad, dumb features revealed confusion.

"I just made that story up—to attract the killer. I was waiting across the street in a car. I figured the person who came looking for the evidence would be the killer."

Melissa looked from Diane to Adam and back again.

Then her features became hard and resolved.

"I don't believe you." She shook her head. "You always tell the truth, Diane. Always!"

"Not this time!" said Adam. "Put down the match, Melissa. There's no evidence to destroy."

Melissa blew out the match, which had nearly burned out anyway.

But then she backed away toward the door.

She drew out another match and lit it.

"I don't know. And I don't want to take the chance."

"Melissa! Don't you think that if you burn this house down, Toni will die too?"

Melissa shrugged. Walking backward, she blew out the match and lit another one. The smell of the burning phosphorus mixed with the smell of gasoline. "Too bad."

"But wait. What if you set the house on fire and Toni gets out! She'll know who threw the match. Don't you think she'll come looking for you?"

That gave Melissa pause.

Something like fear flickered over her features.

Considering this, she shifted her path and backed into an umbrella stand.

She lost her balance and tumbled.

She must have fallen right into a puddle of gasoline because when she dropped the match onto the floor, it instantly caught. Flames raced along the Indian rug, almost immediately connecting with Melissa Birch's sweater.

Which immediately caught flame.

And the flames spread up her arm and across her back.

Horrified, Melissa flung herself against the wall, trying futilely to stamp out the flames.

Her hair caught fire.

She screamed.

Melissa lurched for the front door.

She opened it and ran out onto the porch and into the front yard, the flames blazing up incandescently.

The fire in front of Diane and Adam roared up, catching on to the drapes and creating such a horrible inferno that it cut them off from the front door.

"The backdoor!" said Adam.

"We can't. The fire's in the hallway too!"

"Okay! Then upstairs!"

"Upstairs?"

"Hurry! No time to argue!" He grabbed her arm and pulled her along behind him.

Diane blindly followed Adam, her breath hot in her lungs.

Below them, the growing flames licked at their feet.

16

Just as the flames were consuming the first floor, fear consumed Diane.

Fire!

She was deathly afraid of fire.

Just before they reached the bathroom, Diane realized that she was breathing too hard—hyperventilating, a distant voice thinking inside her head.

A distant voice of herself, totally out of control.

"Adam! Adam!" She gasped, suddenly unable to move further.

Adam spun around. He must have seen the stark terror in her eyes, because he was suddenly full of compassion and understanding.

"Calm down, Diane. Calm down. It'll be okay. I swear it will be okay!"

She took another gasp of air and then *willed* herself to be still, to *stop* this *silliness*.

Immediately, she got control. "I'm okay, Adam. I'll be fine."

"Good." Adam looked up. Smoke was pouring up the stairwell. "We've got to find a way out of here."

A flutter of fire waved upwards toward them like an ephemeral flag.

"Correction," said Diane. "We've got to find a way out of here *fast!*"

"Into the bathroom! Quick!"

Diane needed no encouragement.

The bathroom was much as they left it. Toni Ayers, though, was stirring, groaning, and trying to get up.

Adam leaped into the full tub of water and got himself thoroughly soaked. He pulled himself out. "Okay, you too, Diane."

Diane slipped into the tub, drenching herself again.

When she pulled herself out, she saw that Adam had pulled the groggy Toni up to her feet.

"Gimme a hand," said Adam. Diane jumped out, dripping. She grabbed hold of Toni's feet and helped haul her into the tub. The girl splashed in, her eyes flying open. She floundered about, gasping, caught hold of the sides of the tub and pulled herself, dripping wet out of the huge tub. She blinked out water, took one look at the smoke beginning to pour through the doorway, and said, "What's going on!"

"Fire, Toni," said Adam. "We've got to get out of here!"

Toni started to run toward the door, but Adam grabbed her arm. "Uh uh, Toni. Your buddy spread gasoline all over the place. It's all flames down there."

"Oh jeez. The gasoline . . . that idiot! How do we get out of here?"

Adam was already on that. "There's a window here." He pushed it open and cold air streamed in

165

through fluttering chintz curtains. "The roof's out here. We're going to have to crawl out and then jump down to the ground."

Toni blanched. "That's dangerous!"

"Look, you want to stay here and feed the flames, you're welcome to. Come on, Diane. We're out of here."

Diane didn't have to be persuaded. She walked without hesitation to the window, and crawled out onto the roof.

"Wait!" cried Toni behind her. "No. I'll come."

"You see any pipes out there, Di?" said Adam, helping Toni to clamber out onto the roof.

Diane let her eyes adjust to the dark, and then examined the roof. "Yes. There's one. I don't know how strong it is."

"We're only one story up. Risk it."

Diane pulled herself along the uncertain shingles and then clambered over the edge, groping for balance on the rusty drainpipe.

It creaked and shuddered, but it held.

However, suddenly she slipped on a wet leaf and lost her footing. She grabbed desperately as she fell and managed to hold on to the drainpipe.

It bowed beneath her weight.

"Adam!" she cried. "Help!"

She looked down. Her feet dangled below her.

Yes, it was only one story, but it seemed a *long* way down.

And the ground below wasn't grass; it was a hard cement patio!

"Hang on!" cried Adam. He crept down the roof carefully, extending his hand. "Here, grab hold—"

The dark form came out of nowhere from behind

him. Adam gave an *oooof!* and was pushed out into space.

He dropped like a rock, a surprised yelp streaming down with him.

"Adam!"

He landed on the cement patio with a sickening thud.

He did not get up.

Horrified, Diane looked up. Toni hunkered over her like some drenched bizarre gargoyle, an ugly grin forming on her lips.

"Oops! Too bad, Diane. Looks like your boy-friend kinda slipped, doesn't it!"

"Toni! You *pushed* him!" Her fingers slipped. She pulled up, letting go, and grabbing a firmer hold onto the drainpipe.

"Of course! And now, with luck, he's dead. Which solves one problem. Now I've only got one left." She chuckled. "Namely you!"

"Toni, no!"

Toni carefully reached out with her leg and began crushing Diane's fingers against the gutter with the heel of her shoe.

A bolt of pain jabbed up Diane's arm. With a cry she let go.

She hung on now by one hand.

Precariously.

"There you go! Now we're talking." Toni sneered. She moved her foot over and started pressing against Diane's other hand. "This little piggie went to market, this little piggie stayed home. This little piggie ate roast beef. This little piggie had— NONE!"

Pressed *harder*.

When Diane had taken gymnastics in phys. ed., she had been the absolute despair of her instructor. She'd barely been able to execute a push-up.

However, with her life at stake, she felt the inspiration of desperation.

With every single fiber of her being, she strained upward, flinging up her injured hand.

Despite the pain, she grabbed Toni's ankle and tugged as hard as she could.

Toni was caught off guard. She was pulled off balance. As Diane's hand caught the rim of the gutter again Toni went sailing over her head with a shriek worthy of a witch in a nosedive.

Diane did not watch, but she heard an unhealthy crunch below her as the last of the Evil Sisters hit the cement.

She took a deep breath and began to inch back to the drainpipe and lowered herself slowly to the ground.

17

"Hey, big guy. How are you feeling?"

"Like somebody dumped a truck's worth of bricks on me and then dragged me through a demolition derby by chains—otherwise, just fine."

"Doctor says you'll live."

"Only if you don't break my heart again!"

"Oh, I think we can arrange a truce."

"Sealed with a kiss?"

"Sure."

Diane put down her bouquet of flowers and leaned over the hospital bed and gave Adam a kiss on his black and blue lips.

"Ouch."

"Sorry."

"Hurts so good!" He smiled as she pulled away.

"Never did like that song." She smiled and a tear blurred her vision. "Oh, Adam, I'm *so* glad you're okay. I very nearly lost you."

He tapped the bandages wound around his head. "Nope. This old head is much too hard to break apart easily."

"What's the news on Toni?"

"She's in pretty much the same shape as me."

"Only in a hospital under observation by doctors *and* the cops!"

When the firemen had arrived, brought on by the calls of neighbors, they'd found Melissa's smoking body outside on the front lawn. Help had arrived too late for her.

The house had burned to the ground, while Diane had stood watching helplessly, shivering and only dimly aware of Mrs. Locke's cats weaving restlessly around her legs.

At first, Toni had tried to convince the police that it was Melissa who had killed both the old ladies and Lynn Rivers, but Diane's and Adam's testimony destroyed her story.

"So," Adam said after getting a nice snootful of the flowers she'd brought him. "You going to talk about this in your gossip column?"

She shook her head. "Nope."

"How come?"

"That's another bit of news. I've given up 'Dying to Know'. I devoted this week's column to finding homes for Mrs. Locke's cats, and it was my last gossip column."

"But, Diane! You're such a good writer!"

"I didn't say that I was giving up journalism." Diane laughed airily. "You're looking at the Maxville High *Trumpet*'s new investigative reporter!"

Adam blinked, surprised. Then he groaned. "Does this mean I'm going to have to keep rescuing you from dangerous situations?"

Diane shook her head. "I'm not covering anything deadlier than the food in the Maxville High cafeteria from now on. But anytime you want to rescue me from *that* is fine with me."

"Say with lunch at the Fifties Shack as soon as I'm out of here?"

"It's a date." Diane smiled and leaned over to kiss Adam. There were a lot better things to do with her mouth than gossip, that was for sure.

Spine-tingling Suspense
from Avon Flare

JAY BENNETT

THE DEATH TICKET   **89597-8/$2.95 US/$3.50 Can**
Trouble arrives when a lottery ticket turns up a winner—worth over six million dollars—and maybe more than one life!

THE EXECUTIONER   **79160-9/$2.95 US/3.50 Can**
Indirectly responsible for a friend's death, Bruce is consumed by guilt—until someone is out to get *him*.

CHRISTOPHER PIKE

CHAIN LETTER   **89968-X/$3.50 US/$4.25 Can**
One by one, the chain letter was coming to each of them... demanding dangerous, impossible deeds. None in the group wanted to believe it—until the accidents—and the dying—started happening!

NICOLE DAVIDSON

WINTERKILL   **75965-9/$2.95 US/$3.50 Can**
Her family's move to rural Vermont proves dangerous for Karen Henderson as she tries to track down the killer of her friend Matt.

CRASH COURSE   **75964-0/$2.95 US/$3.50 Can**
A secluded cabin on the lake was a perfect place to study...or to die.